2999 Adler Street

by Arend Wieman

Canadian Cataloguing in Publication Data

Wieman, Arend.
2999 Adler Street

ISBN 1-55212-473-8

I. Title.
PS8595.I53144T86 2000 C813'.54 C00-911195-6
PR9199.3.W472T86 2000

TRAFFORD

This book was published *on-demand* in cooperation with Trafford Publishing.
On-demand publishing is a unique process and service of making a book available for retail sale to the public taking advantage of on-demand manufacturing and Internet marketing. **On-demand publishing** includes promotions, retail sales, manufacturing, order fulfilment, accounting and collecting royalties on behalf of the author.

Suite 6E, 2333 Government St., Victoria, B.C. V8T 4P4, CANADA
Phone 250-383-6864 Toll-free 1-888-232-4444 (Canada & US)
Fax 250-383-6804 E-mail sales@trafford.com
Web site www.trafford.com TRAFFORD PUBLISHING IS A DIVISION OF TRAFFORD HOLDINGS LTD.
Trafford Catalogue #00-0138 www.trafford.com/robots/00-0138.html

10 9 8 7 6 5 4 3 2

Synopsis of 2999 Adler Street

A Vancouver private detective, already in his seventies but still as fit as a man twenty years his junior, meets a much younger woman, a former stripteaser and belly dancer. Although she is doomed by AIDS, he invites her to become his assistant and she actually solves their first case through a dream experience she's had. Eventually they get married and her dreadful disease recedes, dissolved by their great love for each other.

All the violence of today's society, such as murder, kidnapping, sexual abuse, hatred, drug running, racism, child abuse and religious fanaticism, to name only a few of man's negative passions, come to bear in the stories of this exciting novel.

Many of the cases are solved with the assistance of a little dog, displaying an extraordinary fine nose, and outclassing the German Shepherds of the police. There also is a very close relationship between the detective and a police sergeant; in many cases they assist each other, but are trying not to let anybody in on it. Intuition, hunches and a voice from within, often are the tools used to look behind some of the mystery cases and get them unraveled.

However, in spite of all the negativity, violence and abuse, there's also deep love, compassion and humor demonstrated and applied by the leading participants of these stories.

2999 Adler Street
by Arend Wieman
Table of Contents

Prologue

The private detective, Philip Wilbock, in his seventies already, meets a woman, thirty years his junior, and not only does she become his wife, but also his assistant. Their great love for each other began in a former lifetime, as they discovered in one of their dreams. Beautiful Sonja Schilds used to be a stripper and belly dancer, until the terrible disease AIDS devastated her life in more ways than one. However, her new husband with his positive attitude on life, but also on death – telling her that soul is eternal – puts new vigor and decisive consciousness back into his wife. Eventually she's even able to outwit her dreadful ailment.

One of the detective's friends is Sergeant Will Whetherby (later Lieutenant Whetherby) from Vancouver's police headquarters, and the two often work together secretly, assisting each other and solving hopeless criminal cases.

Another dear friend of the private detective is Welda Eisen, whose little dog, Tom, has an extraordinarily sensitive nose, outclassing the German Shepherds of the police by a wide margin.

Several policemen's wives and their friends have begun an organization to assist kidnapped children and their parents, and they call themselves 'The Lost and Found Children's Mission'. The idea came from one of Philip Wilbock's cases, where, by sheer determination, a child was reunited with its father.

Dreams, intuition, inner voices, hunches, love and the psychic, are often the tools used by this private eye with great success, besides the intellectual mind. And, as it looks, age is not slowing down this detective in his endeavor to be of assistance to his fellow men, by curtailing the criminal elements of today's society. Whether it is the intellect or the spiritual, whether the physical or the heart, they're all important aspects of Philip Wilbock's consciousness, and are kept in good working order, and they probably will stay that way for a long time to come.

2999 Adler Street book number I and II are a series of continuous detective stories.

Chapter 1

A Kiss of Trust

At the amusement park inside the Edmonton Mall in Alberta – one of the largest complexes of this kind in the world – a man well advanced in years watched the happy children on one of the merry-go-rounds, enjoying himself, as their jubilant cries awoke 'the child' in him. It warmed his heart and soul, and kindled his great love for them.

A few steps away, a woman in her thirties also had her eyes on the happy young fry, but her beautiful face expressed sadness, although her love was true from the heart. 'If I only could…' her thoughts began, 'if I only had … but time is not on my side.' She took a deep breath, accentuating her emotional pain.

Her next awareness were the man's eyes and smile in her direction. 'Oh, those eyes,' she thought, heavy-hearted, 'so full of love.'

Having come closer to her, he said, "We should be riding with them, but with the long waiting line, we only would take the seats of two longing youngsters."

When she heard his warm words again, they inquired, "What's an attractive young lady doing here, watching the going-ons in this park of enjoyment and laughter?"

"I could ask you the same," she countered. "A gentleman of your age, I can imagine, could find other spots of interest in this giant mall."

"True, true...." His eyes looked deeply into hers, then with an ardent smile he replied, "You see, children are my passion. Not that I want to capture a lost youth again, no, but rather give my love. I want to give love, which has escaped me for the better part of my life, and it is deep-felt love from the heart. Well, children are the easiest recipients."

Now she was facing him, and with a serious tone said, "You're not that old ... I mean ... there should be a woman ... oh, I don't want to prod."

He laughed. "Yes, yes, yes, that sounds like my friends, mostly married women and all much younger. I could rattle down a lot of reasons right here... And pertaining to the young lady facing me, I could point out a few observations. I could ... I could ... it's the old standby. However, we are living in the here and the now at this moment. For instance, I do detect a deep sadness, which not only reflects through your eyes and face ... I can feel it here." And he lifted a hand to his heart. There was no answer and she turned away, so he thought, 'Perhaps she's craving for love, but not the love from this old fellow. The atmosphere between us has become too heavy, I'd better lighten it up.' Then he said, "Would you like to join me for a cup of cappuccino? I saw a little cafe a while ago."

She agreed and while they walked out of the amusement park, he introduced himself: "I'm Philip Wilbock, a vacationing private detective from Vancouver. Call me Phil, please."

"Sonja Shilds," he heard her say quietly, "My friends call me Soshi, but I like Sonja better."

Sipping the steaming coffee at the little table and enjoying it, he finally said, "Having not much to do at the moment, I thought it a good idea to visit this big mall; one hears and reads a lot about it. This is my second day here, and there's simply too much to be seen." He gave her an encouraging smile.

"I'm from Vancouver, too," she began, "and actually wanted to travel across Canada, but kind of got stuck here. Originally I'm from Edmonton; I grew up here. My parents are dead, though, and I was the only child, with no old friends left. The city has changed so much from what I remember, over twenty years back. But this mall is nice … I like it." A moment later, she continued her thought train: "I don't feel like going further east to Toronto and Montreal, where it's probably not too much different from this big indoor shopping center. In a couple of days I might go home again."

With alert eyes, he suggested, "How about a quiet dinner tonight at the McDonald? That's where I stay."

"I stay there, too," she replied, "but already have a dinner date. I've met an old acquaintance I haven't seen for years. Perhaps we'll run into each other at the coast again."

He thought, 'Ah, she wants to get rid of me. Well, physically we two are simply too different. However, there is some part of her beauty, of her … character, that attracts my inner being, more than what I see on the surface.'

Indeed, Sonja Shilds was a very beautiful woman, well built like a model or movie star, with facial features that would prompt any man to turn and have a second look. Her dark brown hair was kept simple and straight, just about reaching her shoulders. Her grey eyes had an attractive depth that one could call 'the eyes of the soul'. Her mouth was well-formed, and a simple movement of her lips could be inviting or rejecting, yet mirror any state of her being. She was easy to read by any good observer, if she could be more relaxed. So, Philip Wilbock had read her right; her face, mind, heart and soul displayed deep sadness, but also fear and helplessness.

Before they parted, Philip said, "I have discovered true love, although late in my life; it's wonderful to give, as I indicated at the carousel with the children. In my philosophy of life, I also discovered other vital ingredients, but not less important when it comes to death, for instance. I can assure you, it's not what our religions and society teaches. If you think this old fellow might have something to offer, please do pay me a visit." And he handed her his card while they got up.

Looking at it for a moment, she said, "Thanks," then

turned quite suddenly and left, a rather cryptic departure.

Philip thought, ' I wonder why she was so short up now? Perhaps she has had some disappointing experiences with men, or I'm simply too old for her.'

Coming back to the hotel late, he soon went to bed. His next awareness was in a dream, walking up the stairs of what looked like a temple entrance, where he was received by an elderly and kind-looking man. He was dressed like a monk and bare-headed; he simply greeted him with the words, "Soul is eternal ... it does not care about age or gender."

'He must be referring to the young lady I met at the mall,' Phil thought, 'and my age difference with her.'

He was led along a well-lit corridor into a room where about twenty people of all ages and races were seated already, apparently expecting a lecture. As if Philip had been the last arrival of the listeners, his guide at once began to address the assembly with gusto: "All the religions of your earth world speak of love, that you can obtain everything with love. Love thy family, love thy friends, thy neighbor, thy enemy, love the whole world and peace will be at hand. And what has this fervent call for love done to your world? Not much, except perhaps save humanity from blundering into total disarray.

"For divine love we must learn to go to <u>soul</u>, and soul, being of the essence of God, is the only agent to give <u>true</u> love.

"However, most of mankind is not aware of its real self, soul; hence their love is not of the highest God order and much less effective.

"To begin with, soul is not able to give love on a grand scale, as suggested by your religious leaders. Soul love is meant to be directed to God first and then given to the closer family and friends. But from the heart you can give good will to all of mankind.

"All of you are conscious of the spark of God within, which is soul, and are able to give its love by applying the positive virtues and self-discipline.

"Be not deceived by sensual love of lower rank, although it has its place in the fulfillment of human existence.

"Let soul be thy overlord in all of your undertakings and be always true to your inner self."

Waking up in the middle of the night, Philip Wilbock remembered every word spoken by the monk in this unusual dream. Aroused into his deepest being from this strange encounter, he lay awake for a long time, the discourse of the dream lecturer made it impossible to go back to sleep.

* * *

Five days later and back in Vancouver, Philip answered the house-bell, and there she stood in her beauty, embarrassed, trying to find the right words. With a deep smile he pulled her in by the elbow, "Please, come on in, Sonja. I thought I recognized you, driving around the block."

Now even more embarrassed, she began to stutter, "I … I … I wasn't sure … I mean —"

"You mustn't be embarrassed, Sonja, please, be at ease with me," he interrupted to take the edge off her discomfort, then steered her into the living room. "And I'm so glad you took me up on my invitation for a visit. I honestly didn't think you would. Now, if we could replace these unruly vibrations between us and replace them with trust."

Suddenly, on the spur of the moment, he had an idea, so, before he seated her, he suggested with determination, "I simply cannot have you in my presence with those fleeting emotions, Sonja; now, will you help me in this endeavor, please? An inner nudge tells me to do it this way." Raising his right index finger to his lips, he pulled her closer and invited her to, "Put your lips on the other side of my finger." Very abashed and reluctantly she did. "That's our <u>kiss</u> <u>of</u> <u>trust</u>! All unmanageable negative feelings between us, are now forgotten."

Out of his grasp and pushing herself away, she suddenly began to cry, only to be embraced and comforted by Philip. Slowly her inner fear dissipated and she began to relax and trust this man. A mysterious inner link seemed to have emerged among the two.

Later, sipping hot coffee in the comfort of their easy chairs, Sonja began to open up slowly, but still had difficulties to convey in words what was on her mind and heart; quietly she revealed, "I'm glad I came; this morning at first, I was afraid. I have a lot to tell and this 'kiss of trust', as you call it, has given me confidence," she gave him a thin smile.

Having finished her brew, she began in her quiet manner, "I have AIDS ... I'm HIV positive. So, you see, I have nothing to look forward to."

Playing with her empty cup, she continued, "I haven't lived a good life ... not that I was a girl who gave sex for money. But I did stripteasing a lot ... a lot, and some of the men took me to bed. It was not what you think, though. I always hoped that one man wanted me for real love and not for his cold desire only. I made good money and the night clubs where I worked were filled with men mostly, paying a high price to see me in action and to see my beautiful body, of course. Their gleaming eyes said it all. I also did belly-dancing, and they said I was the best."

A bit later, with a disgusted laugh, she burst out, "Inevitably, I got the AIDS from one of those men who ... you know what I mean. If I only could've stopped this earlier. I knew in my deepest heart that it was wrong and might backfire eventually. But I refused to be sensible. I also was greedy. I was stupid and lazy, with no discipline." She glared out of the window and her eyes began to blink, then she took a hanky out of her purse to blow her nose into it.

Philip got up and with a motion invited her to sit down beside him on the couch. Putting his hand on hers, he suggested, "First of all, you have to stop feeling sorry for yourself. It's the worst thing you can do and it only will get you deeper into your emotional qualm. If you can, forget about the AIDS for awhile. It looks to me that you're not yet on the physical downward grade, or?"

She shook her head, "I don't feel really sick, not yet anyway. But they say it's only a matter of time, not too far hence."

"Well, forget what they say," he emphasized with a light slap on her hand. "Try to become your own master, and I will help you in this. You must become strong, have a strong self-belief and a trust in the self. Then you must learn to love yourself!" He stressed every word. "Whether you believe it or not, the best tool for this is discipline. Yes, don't shake your head with doubt; by applying discipline you can learn to love and your heart and soul will open and follow. I know, I know, it sounds terribly mechanical, intellectual, without any kind of feeling, but I speak from experience. Today I can turn on love toward a young recipient – or an old one, if open-hearted – and he or she will turn toward me, they feel and know it. The intellect and the mind in a young child is still not developed; that's why it so easily detects this love flow. So it is with young lovers, when they come into each other's orbit, the mind doesn't play any part in it. They feel and know." Then, with an afterthought, he added, "Unfortunately, this love also can be used by people who're only interested in having power over their fellow beings."

Some time later, with a lot of thoughts and feeling behind them, Phil suggested, "Come, let's go into the kitchen and have a sandwich lunch. You're hungry, I hope?"

Nodding, his young companion followed, still having her thoughts on his words. Then, as if suddenly awakened to the present, she prodded. "How do you know all this? I mean, it's not from reading a lot of books and –"

"My line of work as a detective gives me a lot of experiences, Sonja, and often I learn in my dreams, too," he interrupted her. "It's a long story, not told in a few sentences. But, at this moment in time, my knowledge and understanding might be of some benefit to a young lady who thinks she's down on her luck and life."

Eating lunch at the table, Phil finally smiled and said, "Eventually I will tell you all, you can be sure of that. Let's begin with trust; by now you must know that I never could do anything to you, you'd disagree with."

"I know that, Phil; I can feel it deep within me," she assured him in her quiet way.

Looking at her beauty, he nodded contentment, but also felt a hidden yearning. What he would give to be forty years younger again!

Chapter 2

Their First Case

When Sonja came to Philip's place the next day, he said, "I forgot all about the appointment I have with one of my boys. I'm a member of the Big Brother organization; we help youngsters without a father. I'll tell you more later."

Sonja said at once, "I'd better come back then."

"No, no," he countered at once, "you stay right here and make yourself at home. Come with me and I'll show you the house."

Upstairs there were four bedrooms and above that a large attic. After the tour, he suggested, "One of the bedrooms will be yours, so choose one yourself."

With a smile, she replied, "You speak as if I am moving in soon."

"Of course not, but..." he took her arm, while descending the flight of stairs," ... there might be occasions when it's too late to go home."

Entering the large basement, Phil said, "I wish we could stop playing the old theater game between man and woman, Sonja, if you know what I mean; in your old profession you had a lot of that, too. I want to help you very much, but, with any kind of suspicion it's much more difficult. Always remember our 'kiss of trust'. Time and experience will tell what we might become to each other, but it must be positive and happy."

"I'm sorry if I gave you the wrong impression," she apologized.

"No need for that," he assured her, while entering a large exercise room with a lot of workout equipment. "Here I keep fit, but I also have extended walks in parks or a nearby forest. In the next room I have a hot tub, my favorite place. It's always ready to be used. Most of my friends and I don't wear bathing suits, but we have them ready, if somebody doesn't like the idea. So, bring yours next time, please."

Upstairs again, he continued, "most people favor a dining room; in this house, it's all done in the kitchen. But I have a library and a little study. The living room is much larger than normal because it extends outside onto the large porch with a glass wall, as you might've observed already.

"And now I have to go," he added, then patted her on the arm, "there're no secrets here, so, do some exploring, if you wish. I'll be back in about five or six hours. See you then." And he left through the door into the garage.

'I still have to get used to this new relationship with Phil,' she thought, 'he finds it all so natural. 'Was it my fate to meet a man like him eventually? But he is so much older. Maybe I simply should forget any close relationship, certainly with him.'

* * *

One of Phil's Big Brother charges was a boy of six, just about ready to start school after the holidays in a couple of months. His name was Robert and he was waiting outside the house, while his mother looked out of the window. "Hi Phil," she called out, "what are you two up to today?"

Walking toward the house, Phil suggested, "I kind of thought to go to the beach; it's a very low tide." Then, as he had come closer, "Hi, you two, how was your week? I was in Edmonton to see the big mall. We should get together on a rainy day and I'll tell you all about it then."

"Nothing too exciting here," replied Robert's mother, Thea. "I should join you, it should be interesting, with the sea so far out."

"Why don't you?" Phil suggested.

"No, I have an appointment," Thea replied, disappointed; "still looking for a job, you know. Look at him, he's already waiting in your car. Well, have fun ... see you in the late afternoon." She sent the two off with a wave of her hand.

Philip Wilbock sure had a way with youngsters, and six-year-old Robert was no exception. He opened up a world of wonder to him at the beach, using the imagination, creativity and joy. After they had collected several cans full of shells and pebbles, and as the sea water was on the rise again, they walked all the way back into the sand to build a castle, but not before a hearty lunch was eaten. Phil then thought, 'I don't know why the father-child relationship has escaped me most of my life; it seems to come so natural now.' Then, 'Perhaps Sonja is also in that bracket. I sure like her and we two seem to hit it off right. I wonder what we can do about her AIDS? I hate to see her dying in my arms. So young and already so much experience in her night club jobs. A lot of karma there.'

"Uncle Phil," he heard the boy holler, "I'm getting the sand together. Are you finished eating?"

It was an afternoon of laughter and also diligence to get their creation completed, then many of the shells were placed on all the important points of the sand structure, with Robert's name in the middle of it to give the castle an expensive look. Finally, a young lady, who happened to wander along the beach, took a picture with the two standing behind their creation.

"I'll bring the picture next time," Phil called out, as he let the youngster off at his home. Waving good-bye to his mother, he drove off, a very happy man, filled with the day's events. Yes, this was his life, one he created himself.

* * *

He hardly had closed the large garage door, when Sonja greeted him excitedly with a smile in the opened doorway of the kitchen. "You'll never guess what I did and what got me so aroused?"

"I bet you took a hot bath and liked it a lot," he suggested, taking her hand.

“Well, that, too,” she replied, as they entered the kitchen. “No, it’s rather … I don’t know whether I should’ve done it. It’s your private … I read your dream records,” she said, rather nervous, watching his reaction.

“Aha,” he said with a grin, “so you have been in my bedroom.”

“You said there were no secrets, and I was nosy, so I…” she tapered off, obviously embarrassed. “I couldn’t stop reading it, Phil.”

As they entered the outside porch through the opened living room glass door, to enjoy the sun, he put an arm around her waist and turned her slightly in his direction, then said, “You may relax, young lady. Although very private at times, the dream log puts you right in the middle of all I’m involved with and believe in. So, having read it all –”

“No, I didn’t,” she interrupted quickly. “Every time I came to a private and sensitive part, I stopped reading and went on to the next. I swear, Phil, I didn’t read those parts.”

When he saw a few tears running down her cheeks, he comforted her with, “I believe you, Sonja. Actually, I’m glad you read it. I was thinking about how to expose you to all this spiritual business, if I may call it that. Now you have made it rather easy, by taking the initiative, and you like it, I presume?”

“Do I? Oh, Phil,” she burst out, “I love it! But there are many things I don’t understand.”

“Simmer down,” he counseled, seating himself beside her on the swinging couch, “and I will tell you all.”

A few moments later he suggested, “Now you also might understand why we two hit it off so well, so easily. There’s not much doubt in my mind anymore today that we’ve been together in a past lifetime, perhaps as father and daughter, brother and sister, adversaries, or even as lovers. We’ve been in both genders. All those old experiences we have brought with us, imprinted in the present day karma, it’s the law of cause and effect. If it isn’t resolved in a past lifetime, it’ll be tabled again now, to be worked out, or not. The choice is with us.”

Then, pulling her off the couch, he led her toward the

kitchen, saying, "And now we'll prepare supper; I have a certain casserole in mind and it needs an hour in the oven."

"With you, Phil," she watched him at work, chopping up vegetables and meat, "my AIDS is almost forgotten. It hung so heavy over me, and I was so listless, so discouraged and fearful. But now..."

He replied, "But now you know already that our soul is the real you, me and everybody else, too; that the body is just a vehicle we need in this life."

"But I like my body, Phil," she said rather seriously.

"So do I! There is nothing wrong with that," he agreed with her. "It's often a slow process to shift the attention away from the physical and material; it's an art. But at least the whole death affair is put into a different light. Soul is eternal, you understand; it goes from lifetime to lifetime."

At that moment the telephone rang and, having the speaker on, they both could hear the voice. "Is this 2999 Adler Street? I hear you're a good detective," they heard a man's forceful tongue.

"You're only good solving a case," Phil replied.

"That's true enough," came the assured answer, "so, I want to hire you."

Phil quickly had his say first. "By the way, our conversation over the phone is recorded. I charge $150 an hour or $350 a day. I also like my privacy, with no police still on the case. No talk to friends or to the press. If any of these rules are broken, I'm off."

The man's voice came back at once, "All that is agreeable to me. Money is no problem and if you solve the case, there will be a bonus."

Phil's answer was quick: "I don't work with bonuses; only my fee, please."

"All right," came the voice back, "all right. It's about the disappearance of my daughter and granddaughter you might've –"

"Is that the Waterton case?" Phil interrupted. "I know much about it through the papers. I'll take it. In the meantime, no calling, please. I'll call you as I proceed, okay?"

"Sounds good." The man said, satisfied. "Good luck." And he hung up.

"With all the detective work you're doing," Sonja commented, "no wonder you're so knowledgeable in all that other stuff, too."

With his hands dripping, Phil asked Sonja, "Please, press the button under Sergeant Whetherby. He is my contact with the police. It's not known by the public, though, so, no word of it gets out of this house."

It was her introduction into his real life.

"Police headquarters," crackled a woman's voice over the phone speaker.

"Is Sergeant Whetherby in?" Phil asked.

"Who's calling?" the woman asked. "Is that you, Phil? I recognize your voice. Don't worry ... my lips are sealed. The sarge just went out for lunch."

"It must be you, Erika," Phil replied. "Have him call me, first opportunity. Thanks, old pal. Anything new in your life?"

"Not that I know of," came the laughing voice back. "I'll let you know. And you?"

He also laughed. "You might not believe this, but I've got a very young lady here now, finding deep interest in me; in fact, she's sitting right here." He grinned at Sonja.

That caused another muffled laugh over the phone, "You better watch that old-young guy; he's still loaded with vigor ... hey, I've got to go." And she hung up.

Disappointed, Sonja commented, "That probably means we won't see each other for at least a week."

"Nooo, nooo, my dear lady..." Phil grinned with a hidden meaning. "We two shall take this case together."

"But ... but ... I'm not ..." she stuttered.

"It'll be a different experience from what you know, Sonja." He patted her arm. "Would you like to?"

"But what qualifications do I have?" The question surged out of her.

Phil said very determined, "Don't worry, I'll teach you, and the in betweens you pick up on the run."

"You make it sound so easy, Mister detective," Sonja aired her worry.

"In this business nothing is easy," Phil looked deeply

into her eyes. “Are you with me?”

“Yes,” she replied, holding his eyes steady.

Sonja thought, ‘From a stripteaser to a detective’s assistant, quite a change; but I trust him to be easy on me.’

“I think you’ll do all right.” Philip reflected.

* * *

When the phone rang again, it was Sergeant Whetherby and he asked, “What’s up, Phil?”

“What have you got on the Waterton case, Will?” he inquired, “can I see the bodies and some pictures?”

“I see he took my hint. Strong-minded, you know. How about in half an hour at the morgue on my way home?” the sergeant suggested.

“Sounds good to me,” Phil agreed. “By the way, I have a young assistant with me. See you then.”

Scooping up his old detective bag, he guided Sonja through the garage door and they got into the car and drove off to their gloomy destination.

At the morgue entrance, Sergeant Whetherby couldn’t take his eyes off Phil’s escort. ‘I wonder where he picked her up?’ he marveled.

After shaking hands and entering the large underground hall, the sarge thought, ‘Don’t tell me she knows anything about our business.’ Then aloud said, “Here, have a look at the pictures.” And he handed them over to his friend.

With the bodies taken out of the coolers, Phil pulled the coverings off and began to look closely with his magnifying glass at the wounds. He finally said, “The head wounds probably indicate the usage of a blunt hammer. The stab wounds on the woman’s chest go from right to left, a right-handed killer, I’d say; but on the girl it’s from left to right … Two persons could’ve done it.”

Phil got out a steel wire probe and inserted it into the wounds. “You see, Sarge, how far it goes inside the flesh, almost a foot. It must’ve come out the back of the girl; let’s roll her over. See, right under the skin there, almost through. They must’ve used a special knife with a thin, long blade to almost penetrate the chest.” The sergeant just nodded.

Phil continued, "The hammer probably was used to knock them unconscious first. What do you say, Will?"

"You've opened a couple of new avenues, Phil." The sergeant scratched his head. "Something to pursue."

"What else have we got?" Phil asked.

By now Sonja had become so white-faced and ill, that she had to grasp for a chair, the observant morgue keeper had put behind her. He also gave her a glass of water.

Very concerned, Phil asked, "Sonja! Are you all right, girl? I forgot all about you. Maybe you want to go outside?"

"I'm okay now, Phil," she replied. "Just let me sit here for a moment."

The curious sergeant whispered, "Should you have brought her, Phil? Obviously, she's not cut out for this work."

Breathing deeply, Phil answered, "She will be, in time. Now then, what else have we got?" he asked as he continued the examination. "What's in there, Will?" he pointed to a container.

"In this bag we have four cigarette butts, and they are all Camels," the sergeant said, with assurance.

"Did you get them tested?" Phil asked. "Only one shows that it's a Camel. If there were two people ... you see what I mean?"

"Yes, you're right, Phil ... I'll have them tested, first thing in the morning." Will patted his old friend on the shoulder. "Knowing you..." he did not finish. Then he whispered once more, "Who's she anyway? A friend or relative? A secret, hey?"

"She needs my help, Will," was Phil's answer. "You can call her a friend. Come, I'll introduce you."

"Sonja, the sergeant wants to meet you," Phil said, then he introduced them. "Might as well ... you are going to see more of each other."

Grinning, they shook hands before parting.

It had become late and at home Phil suggested, "Perhaps we can watch a short movie, then you sleep over."

"How can you be so relaxed with those two dead ... a little girl only?" Sonja tried to understand her companion's detached state of mind and emotions.

"Years of experience ... or you become a nervous wreck," Phil explained. "You can see that, can't you?" Then he asked, "Did you ever see the movie, Schindler's list?"

"No, and I don't want to see it either," was her rather stern reply. Then, almost whispering, she added, "I'm a Jew, Phil." She watched his reaction.

"That's a good enough reason, I think," was his rather sober answer. "I can imagine that not everybody wants to be reminded. And often relatives and friends have been murdered in those damn camps. It's a good movie, however, for many of today's young people to see. Those events of over fifty years back are too easily forgotten, unfortunately. The violence seems to increase every year."

"I wouldn't mind getting into the hot tub," Sonja suggested, obviously wanting to change the subject.

"What a splendid idea!" Phil exclaimed immediately. "I'd like that myself. Come, I'll find a bathing suit for you."

* * *

The morning, shortly after five, the master of the house prepared his breakfast and skimmed over the local newspaper while eating on one of the high stools at the counter.

It must have been two hours later when Sonja rushed into the living room and called out, "I know where the weapons are located! I saw it in my dream!"

"Okay, okay," Phil said, patting beside him, "sit down and tell me. But why not have breakfast first?"

"No, Phil!" she said excitedly, "I might forget it again." Having calmed down, with him beside her, she began to explain, "There was a little pond right under a bent-over palm tree and in it is a plastic bag with a knife <u>and</u> a hammer. I saw it, Phil."

"That's all?" Phil called out, having expected much more. "And now we know exactly where to look, my beautiful dreamer." With a deep breath he added, "Look, girl, there are no palm trees like that up here in the north."

"I know, I know," she struggled to explain, "but if there should be a tree like that here in Vancouver, it would be easy to find because it's so exceptional. It was bent like one of those coconut trees in Hawaii, something like a bow. We could look, Phil."

"Hmmmm ... perhaps you have something there, my smart little assistant ..." He patted her on the hand. "Maybe the dream wasn't for nothing."

He got up to get the telephone book. "Who could we call for more information? How about the park superintendent? He might know more."

"The only tree of this nature, the way you describe it," they heard the man's voice over the phone speaker, "you might still find in the university park, if they are still there. It must've been over ten years ago when I saw them last time."

An hour later the two were cruising along the seashore, several times back and forth, but saw nothing, so Phil finally suggested, "While we're here, we might as well zigzag the whole university ground."

Then driving past a large storage shed, Sonja suddenly called, "Phil, Phil, look there. Turn around and drive in there." As they came around the corner, she cried with excitement, "That's the tree I saw! Exactly, Phil, there's no doubt!"

"And there is the little pond," Phil remarked dryly. 'Her dream could be a gold mine,' he thought, but before he could suggest anything, she already was out of the car and up to her knees in the water, trying to find the bag with her bare feet.

Phil had watched a guard come closer, obviously not liking their activity, when he heard Sonja cry out, "I've got it! I've got it!" and with her hand she scooped up a plastic bag out of the murky water.

"What do you think you're doing there?" They heard the irate voice of the guard. "Come out of there immediately or I'll call the police!"

"Yes," Phil agreed happily, "call Sergeant Whetherby at Police Headquarters." He said that while putting his arm around Sonja and taking the bag with deep satisfaction and joy. "That was great work, Sonja," he whispered into her ear, and it showed her pride.

The guard was satisfied, after Phil had presented his

detective credentials.

At home, Phil put his hand around her waist once more and, with an impish grin said, "Maybe some day we'll find a way to kiss, without taking a chance of getting the AIDS." It really made her blush.

* * *

When Detective Wilbock got Sergeant Whetherby on the phone he said, with a smile of satisfaction toward Sonja, "You'd never guess what we found, old boy?"

"Well…" came the slow answer, "going by your voice, and with a smart new assistant now, my experience is telling me you found the weapons."

"Yes, Will, we did!" was the joyful answer. "But you'd never guess how we went about it."

"Knowing you, Phil," came Will's answer back, "I bet it was by your intuition."

"No, not this time, Will," Phil replied, "but, believe it or not, it was through Sonja's dream."

"Okay, okay," was his impatient answer, "what do you expect me to say … that I believe you? And what do I write into my report, Phil?"

"Come on now, Will, we've always found a way," Phil said, disappointed. "I just thought you'd like to know how it really happened. I could've told you a wild story, but, as a friend…"

"Sometimes I wish you would, Phil," he said with a deep laugh. "This office is run by normal human beings who go by facts. Well, I'm just in a bad mood today. Hey, we also found that the cigarette butts were two brands, so, there must've been two murderers. In about an hour I could be at your place."

"How about having lunch here, Will?" Phil invited.

"Sounds tremendous," he agreed, then hung up.

While the three ate their sandwiches with great satisfaction and Will had his beloved bottle of beer, he finally began to talk about the case. "Now then, I've already found a way to write this into my report, I don't even want to know how it happened in your dream, Sonja. We have the weapons now and with the fingerprints on them, the rest should be a cinch."

Indeed, the fingerprints put the finishing touches

quickly to this terrible crime and, shortly thereafter, two aircraft workers were arrested. They had known the divorced woman, but when she didn't comply with their carnal desires, they had driven her with the little girl out into the bushes, where they committed the murder in this awful fashion.

The papers were full of the case, but neither Phil's nor Sonja's name were mentioned, which is what they wanted. It was the detective's special understanding with the police.

A few days later, when their minds and emotions had quieted down again, Philip said to Sonja, "I wanted you to experience this. As young as you are, already you have to face death. If your AIDS can't be cured, perhaps I can make it easier for you to look that old man with the scythe in his hooded face, by seeing all this violence I so often come in contact with during my work." He patted her hand with a congenial nod.

Then, after having walked a few steps back and forth, he suggested, "Perhaps this almighty power, or spirit – I so often come to know during my dreams and other unexplainable insights – has brought us two together for reasons we really don't know yet. Your excellent dream revelation, however, was proof to me that we indeed might do well in each other's company." He gave her a deep grin. "Our future will bear that out, as my intuition tells me." Their eyes met with happiness and she thought, with a hand to her heart, 'By God, I think I love this man.'

Chapter 3

The Help of a Shrewd Goat

Philip Wilbock had been busy over the weekend with his two Big Brother charges, Treavour and Hans, but came home Sunday late in the afternoon, disappointed, because Hans' mother had started an argument, accusing him of being a bad father figure, among other things. 'That's a first,' Phil thought, 'perhaps she wants to get rid of me.'

Finally then, feeling sad for the boy, because, of all the boys, this one needed a man's assistance most, Phil said to her, "I know I'm not perfect, and I'm still learning myself, but do you want to talk to my caseworker? She might come up with a better solution, a better man."

"I will do that," she answered at once, and closed the door in front of him.

Coming home, Phil already had his mind on going out to eat, when he heard Sonja's welcome voice over the phone, "Oh, Phil, I simply have to speak to you. Somebody painted the Star of David on my door. How did they know?"

He calmed her down with the words, "It's probably nothing serious. A prank … maybe somebody found out through your old activities." Then, "Want to eat out with me? I'll pick you up in an hour."

Later, climbing into his car, Phil said with a smile,

"Don't make too much out of it. Has it happened before?"

"No," she announced somberly.

"You see," he comforted her, "just a prank."

He parked at a small fish restaurant and asked, "Feel like fish tonight?" She just nodded.

They hardly spoke, but felt comfortable in each other's presence.

An hour or so later, inside the car again, she asked, "Can I stay overnight?"

He felt that there still was some uneasiness in her and immediately said, "Of course." Then, "How about I give you a key, Sonja, and you come whenever you like?"

For a moment she watched him from the side, then said, "I'd like that, Philip." And she put her hand on his arm to give him a squeeze of appreciation.

They hardly had entered Phil's house when the phone rang. "We need a detective to locate my –"

A man's voice then cut off the woman with, "My wife's father is missing and we want him back!" he harshly demanded.

Then they gave their address, and requested a visit in the morning.

Phil commented, "Did you hear the dominance in his tone? I dislike that kind of person. They always interfere. They think they know everything better."

They finished the evening in front of the TV set watching a movie.

* * *

In the morning, the two drove along the Vancouver Island ferry highway, toward the Horseshoe Bay terminal. To their right the home developments climbed high up into the forest, part of West Vancouver. One of the houses up the sloping hillside was their goal.

Having found the place, they left the car to enjoy the beautiful sight over the Burrard Inlet. But soon a man's voice interrupted their interlude of tranquility with the harsh words: "Are you the detective?"

Phil hardly had time to answer when the loud voice continued the dialogue, not having the slightest intention of asking them in, telling them that his wife's father had escaped a hospital where he had been institutionalized. “We let him visit us, but he’s not right up here,” he went on, pointing to his head. “Then he runs away, up into that forest....” He waved his hand toward the higher, sloping area. “That was over a week ago and he’s probably dead by now. We have to know, though, because of the large inheritance.”

Phil thought, ‘That’s straightforward enough, laced with a lot of greed. Now he expects us to climb up that mountain and search for the body. This man gives me the creeps.’ But Phil saw a good hike on the other side of the coin, mixed with some adventure perhaps. So he agreed, much to the surprise of Sonja.

Having entered the wooded area, and out of the man’s hearing, Sonja said with great pain in her voice, “I don’t understand why you accepted it. This is for a forest ranger, Phil, not for us; not for me anyway.”

“Calm down, my beautiful friend,” he said with a smile, taking her hand and patting it. “To begin with, I try never to be the effect of people like that, they’re loaded with anger, and that can spill over on you, if you react,” he gave a short laugh. Then he continued, “Besides, we’ll kill two birds with one stone, having a nice hike in the green environment and looking for a body that doesn’t even exist, to begin with. Furthermore, he’s paying, so cheer up, girl.”

They entered the forest with tall trees towering above them, and might’ve walked for half an hour on the well-worn path, when a friendly goat joined their company. It always kept ahead of them, though, not coming too close, as if it wanted to lead the way. “Oh, this is going to be fun,” Phil called out, inhaling deeply.

In an hour, and several rests along the way, Sonja, hanging onto Phil, said hoarsely, “I’ve had it. You’re wearing good shoes for this, but my feet are sore.”

“Okay, okay,” he comforted her, “perhaps I was too thoughtless, I can see your point. So, make yourself comfortable in this clearing, until I join you again in an hour or two. I simply have to find out where this friendly goat will be leading me.”

“But, Phil,” Sonja lamented, “all by myself here in the wild? If an animal should –”

“What animal?” he interrupted her. “There’re only birds around here and they will keep you company.”

She wanted to say more, but Phil left no doubts, so she sank back into the grass and watched him disappear among the bushes and tall trees.

While walking along faster now, without the frequent rests Sonja needed, Phil lost track of time and any concern for his partner as he mounted the ridge soon. There, three to four hundred feet away, a little log cabin came into view. ‘That’s probably the home of this friendly goat I’m following,’ he thought.

As he approached the old shed, not expecting any human inhabitation at all, a loud shot rang out, making him drop to the ground instantly. ‘That’s odd,’ he thought, ‘I didn’t hear any bullet whistle through the air. Was that just a warning?’

Keeping very low and his eyes on the clearing of the little shelter, he finally came face to face with a wild-looking man, cradling the goat for comfort, as he stared at Phil in anxious anticipation. An old shotgun was lying on the ground, so Philip simply approached him with a deep smile. ‘Oh, this man is shaking all over,’ he thought. ‘He might be the greedy man’s father-in-law, thinking I’m the police to pick him up.’

Phil just looked at him for awhile with friendliness and an open heart, his thoughts and vibrations conveyed nothing but good will.

The next move of the two men was beyond any intelligent understanding as they slowly put their arms around each other, the move seemed to have come so natural.

An hour or so must’ve gone by, with the detective trying to find out, in vain, more about this poor man, who only spoke Russian, with very little English, when Sonja burst into view, exhausted and in tears.

“And I thought you might’ve been wounded or worse even, when I heard the shot,” she cried out, “so I couldn’t stay down there with you up here.”

“Oh, my beloved woman,” Phil comforted as he took her into his arms. “No doubt your adrenaline must’ve given you the tremendous strength to make it up here.”

To give her comfort in her physical and emotional plight, he held her tight for awhile.

Then, after they had seated themselves on an old wooden bench, Phil tried to explain that this man was probably the one they were looking for. “I wish I knew Russian, it’s the only language he speaks.”

Suddenly Sonja got into the act and slowly conversed with the deeply disturbed man. He explained that they had tried to put him away into a mental institution, but he was not crazy, rather the opposite. Then his whole and very sad story unraveled, that even his own daughter was trying to put him away in this awful fashion, to be able to put her hands on his money.

Surprised, Phil asked his mate, “I didn’t know you spoke Russian?”

“I don’t, but my parents came from Poland,” she explained, “and they taught me in my early years. Polish and Russian are somewhat related.”

“You sure saved the day, my wonderful assistant.” With a grin he gave her a hug. “Now we’d better get back to civilization. I guess you’ve really had it, hey?”

“No more walking for me, Phil, not with those shoes.” She leaned back against the cabin wall, looking the other way, while massaging her sore feet.

* * *

Philip had made his way down the other side of the mountain to a small settlement they had been able to see through the tall trees from above. Entering the very first house there it came to bear that the two oldest daughters had discovered the wild-looking but friendly man on one of their weekend hikes. Several times during the week then they had gotten some food, via the very smart goat – most of the older children had played with at times – to Stan Rezausoff, the name of the half-starved man. Before Phil phoned the police, the family offered their help in any way they could. “Would you make him some sandwiches please? He is hungry as a wolf,” the detective requested.

The West Vancouver police sergeant didn’t know what to make of the whole situation, as it was out of his jurisdiction, in spite of Phil’s pleas to find some means to get his friend and the old man off the mountain. "Honestly, I'm very much beat myself and not in much of a position to go up there again, with some food for the old man, and then bring them down," Phil said, inhaling deeply with disdain of the situation he got himself into.

Suddenly then, he had an idea, and said, "Forget about it, sergeant, I'm going to phone my friend at the downtown police; thanks anyway," and he put the receiver down.

"Hey, Will, I sure can use some help now," Phil tried to explain his awkward position, excitedly.

"Hang on for a minute," came his friend's answer, and he could hear several voices in the background. A few moments later, he heard the sergeant's voice again. "You're in luck, old boy, so you can simmer down. The R.C.M.P. (Royal Canadian Mounted Police) will take care of you with a helicopter. That should solve your problem for the moment." Then he added with much disgust, "By the way, Sonja's crazy door painter has struck again ... much worse this time. See you."

In about thirty minutes an R.C.M.P. helicopter swooped down on a small parking lot in this forest community to pick up the delighted detective, and the first words the corporal pilot said with a slight grin, "You must've a lot of pull with the higher-ups in the police force."

Stunned for a moment, Phil laughed heartily, then replied, "There is no pull involved, although this is a first, as far as I'm concerned. However, I will tell you, we always had a good relationship, based on good ethics, among others." Then Phil said, "In two weeks we have a party at my place, where many of my police friends and their families will be present, so come on and find out what we're all about. Bring your lady; here is my card."

As anxious as Sonja was to get out of the wilderness, Stan Rezausoff seemed to be wary, not knowing what might be facing him, but Phil tried to calm him by saying, "Tell him, Sonja, that from now on we will see that he gets his proper care." They also took the gun, for the police to secure.

Landing on the hospital roof and being loaded onto a stretcher, didn't make it any better. Phil could feel the man's apprehension and patted him on the shoulder with a friendly nod, to let him know that he would be alright.

Next day, Phil and Sonja were back to visit the old man with a collection of beautiful flowers and also to find out where he exactly stood financially, what means he might have to live on his own and turn it over to a good lawyer. As it turned out, his own daughter and son-in-law had almost cheated him out of what amounted to a little fortune, he easily could live on for the rest of his life. However, what that man really wanted was love, a true love, what not even his own child was able to give, as she too was blinded by greed.

Shamelessly, Phil asked to be paid a thousand dollars for their mountain and forest excursion, and he got it, too, after he told them, "We found him alive and in poor shape. The R.C.M.P. brought him then with a helicopter to a hospital to recuperate and be looked after by an attorney."

* * *

"Obviously, this man takes great pain to hurt you personally," Phil said to Sonja at home the next day. "It's not so much against the Jews or against AIDS. Unless … he himself is trying to profit from what he does." Phil poked his left index finger to his chin in deep thought.

During her absence the slogan, 'STRIPPERS AND AIDS WILL SUFFER', had been sprayed on the entrance door of her suite.

"People like that become careless in their personal anger," Phil continued, more to himself. Then, after giving it some more thought, he added, "We shall set a trap every night, as long as it takes." He was trying mainly to cheer up his worried companion and get her to relax again.

But the 'animal' sprang the trap much faster than they had anticipated. Phil had it all set up and when this man appeared with his spray bottle during the same evening, Sonja phoned the police, while the wise detective snapped at least a half a dozen pictures, right in the act of vandalism.

As it turned out, this man worked for the largest Vancouver newspaper as a stand-in reporter and wanted to create a big story, he then could cover himself. He was fired of course, but only had to pay a fine for his act, which was not the end of this account either. He managed to get a story into another paper, revealing that Sonja with her AIDS was living with a Big Brother in the same house.

"He really must've done some snooping," the detective was telling his mate. "And that will be the end of my Big Brother job," he suggested dryly. He hardly had the words out, and the president of that organization was on the line. After some pleasantries, she said, "You probably read the paper, too, and know why I am calling. True or not, we –"

Phil cut her short: "I'll save you the details ... I understand."

Sonja put her arms around her mate, and so they stood for a long, long time; they still had their love.

Phil did not let himself become angry – he was beyond that – but the detective in him went to work. "I will do something I never did before," he vowed. "This man doesn't seem to have any scruples and his ethics are practically nil."

Sonja said, "Aha, your revenge is going to work."

"No, my dearest one," he replied, "the word revenge does not exist in my dictionary anymore, I just want to give this guy something to think about. First, he uses you to get ahead, and when his scheme doesn't work, he's trying to get even. Then he involves me in the process, and that was his mistake.

It was easy enough to find the 'door artist's' home, and so Phil snooped around in the neighborhood where he found a very talkative woman, the landlady of this man's fiancée. Apparently she had tried to persuade her lover to come home with her, out east to Saskatoon in Saskatchewan, as she was very homesick.

So the detective intercepted the young lady, as she was walking home from work, introduced himself, and then spoke to her about the shabby activities of her fiancée. "I don't care about myself," Phil said finally, "but look where it left my lady friend and the three boys who have to do without a Big Brother now."

It was obvious, the girl had become very upset and

only was able to utter the words, "That he did that…" The detective couldn't help but feel sorry for her.

However, the results from this conversation on the street with the girl surprised even Phil, namely, in only two days the young couple had left town in the direction of her home in Saskatoon.

Coming home with the news of the man's departure, Phil said to his mate with a relaxed smile, "I don't know what really happened behind the scenes between the two young people. Hopefully, the girl's love will influence him to a more positive life."

A bit later Sonja exclaimed, "Oh, Phil, in spite of all the damage he's done, we can now love each other in peace again."

With a sudden reaction to that, Phil said, "We also can love Stan… Hey, let's buy some flowers and visit him right now at the hospital."

There was a big surprise in store for them. Their wild 'mountainman' was out of bed and without any kind of a beard. His smiles went from ear to ear and his thanks were endless. A good lawyer, speaking his own language, was looking after him now.

Back in the car, Phil reflected once more on the case, and he said, "Results like this all by themselves, make my occupation worthwhile, and I don't mind to go on a long hike into the forest and up the mountain." He gave a deep grin to Sonja.

"Well…" she began, "it was a good lesson for me, Phil; I will improve and certainly need <u>better</u> shoes!"

Later, at home again, Phil suggested, "And now we shall concentrate on your AIDS."

On my AIDS?" she called out surprised.

"Well, of course," he said, "it must be <u>your</u> AIDS, because I haven't got AIDS." They both laughed and she commented, "I completely have forgotten it."

So, over the next few days, they bought and read a lot of books and researched what could be done about Sonja's dreadful disease, away from the so-well-known conventional means. To their surprise, they discovered that it was a very vast subject, but vowed to give it a good fight.

Chapter 4

The Party

"I want you to have a look at my little gun collection," Philip said, inviting Sonja to a cabinet he had opened. "As you know, I seldom use a weapon, but have one ready, in case of danger. This small pistol here is especially made for a woman's hand and it is powerful enough to kill if aimed at the heart or the head. I want you to have it and then carry it for emergencies."

Phil put the holster on her and locked the cabinet door again. On the kitchen table he took the little weapon apart and showed her how to load the magazine. "You have to learn how to shoot it and I already spoke with Sergeant Whetherby, who gave permission to use their shooting range."

For the next few days they practiced at the police facility until Sonja had become a reasonably good shot. "Remember, that thing might save your … our lives, but we only seldom go out consciously depending on it. We're not like the TV people, where the characters are always involved in violent action."

* * *

A few days later, Philip Wilbock began his preparation for the yearly party, he had initiated many years back at his place, inviting close neighbors and friends. Small amounts of wine, beer and barbecue provisions (salmon this year) would be provided by the host, but everybody was chipping in also to make it a successful get-together.

Early in the morning Phil hammered a wooden sign to a post on the front lawn, under the observant eyes of Sonja, and it read: 'The essences of pure heart and soul are the ingredients at this gathering. Religion, politics mustn't apply.'

"Do they all stick with that?" Sonja asked.

"Find out," he teased, grinning.

Several high school boys took it upon themselves to park the cars for the party, so it always worked out, since Philip's property and house was adjacent to a large playground.

The corpulent owner of a restaurant, George Ray, always worked the open charcoal pit, where he was busy already getting the fire going, just to the right temperature. The women in the kitchen had cleaned and washed the twelve large salmon, which were lined up to be put on the grill at the right time.

There always was somebody to look after the thirty or so children, who would have their fun on the playground later, after their stomachs had been satisfied.

Phil was saying to Sonja, "There are usually three or four Bobs, Bills, Margarets and even another Phil at the party ... well, you'll have your fun with it."

When the first plates began to fill and the inviting salmon aroma lingered in the air, the host tapped his fork to a glass of wine to get everyone's attention, then said, "Every year I see a couple of new faces, so perhaps we've got a good thing going here." There was loud applause.

"Last year I promised a chicken party, but was not able to lay my hands on enough of the good range fowl. So, the salmon took their place, right off a fisherman's boat." Again loud applause.

"I would like to introduce my young partner here, and her name is Sonja. In part you already were introduced to her through the busy papers a few weeks back, so, no use going over it again. Please, do your own introductions. Hey, aren't the gods taking personal care of our weather again?" And he followed with the thumbs-up sign and the cheers of everybody; their happiness was evident.

Slowly Phil then 'worked' his way toward his old friend Sergeant Whetherby. Tapping him on the shoulder from behind, he whispered, "I'm kind of curious, Will, how this R.C.M.P. (Royal Canadian Mounted Police) helicopter materialized so quickly, to pick us up just at the right time?"

Grinning deeply, Will answered, "There happened to be two 'higher-ups' in my office at the time, to discuss a very important matter. Well, one of them particularly has a warm spot in his heart for you, and he took care of the situation forthwith. That's all I can tell you, Phil." And he gave him a big grin.

"How is the family, Will? I guess they're all here and doing their 'thing'?"

"Yes, good old Wanda, as usual, loves the kitchen work. Later on she would like a few words with you. I see, Miss … what's-her-name, is getting herself filled up again and just about has had it."

"Oh yes, Miss Hansen," Phil mused. "I don't know how she's able to 'crash' this party every year; she lives over two blocks away and is not invited. She hardly eats anything, just gets drunk." Then, "I think it's just about time now to get her home."

"Let me take care of her," Will said dryly. "So seldom I get out of my office and do some street work; now here is my opportunity." He laughed, then walked off.

Besides the sergeant, there were at least a dozen other policemen at the party, many of them Phil's old acquaintances, who valued his friendship, and also his help on the beat. It seemed that Phil knew most of their families and, as he made the rounds, had laughs with them. Sonja had a good time, too, and enjoyed being accepted by everybody.

Suddenly, though, a man's raised voice challenged her: "I understand you have been deeply into the art of belly dancing," and he made a few funny motions with his hips, enough time for Phil to catch on, although he was on the other side of the garden. The loud voice continued, "Now then, we wouldn't mind seeing some of this demonstrated right now, young lady, or am I asking too much?" He looked around the circle for support.

Needless to say, Sonja was deeply embarrassed and any kind of an answer got stuck in her throat. The whole garden party then came to a halt, and nobody said a word, all looking in that direction.

Everybody seemed relieved when Phil arrived on the scene, knowing his composure in situations of this nature. For a long time he looked at the man, and also noticed his wife's mortified face, deeply ashamed of her husband's words.

When Phil finally spoke, his words came out slowly and with strength, "I wonder, Dennis, whether you've read the sign in front of the house, meaning we leave the negative passions at home, if there are any. If you had too much to drink, I'll have to ask you to leave this party. If it was just an unintentional slip of the tongue, we're willing to look the other way and accept your apology."

However, Dennis Blackwell, the owner of a large furniture store, rather chose to make a fool of himself and burst out: "Heck, I'm not drunk, Phil. What's wrong with asking an honest question? She was a belly dancer, we all know that. I've seen her myself. Why not have her perform here? Or are we all puritans at this party? Hey? Hey?" And he looked around himself, expecting everybody's agreement.

There was not an iota of a rush to Phil's words, when he said, "You have made your choice, and we've made ours." He took Sonja's arm and left the scene. Two minutes later, a red-faced Dennis, urged by his wife, left the party.

George, the restaurant owner, called from the barbecue pit: "We all know where we stand, don't we?" And there was loud applause with cheers.

Once more Phil got their attention, when he said, "Yes, we do know … I trust we all do. So, I will tell you because it is true; Sonja was a belly dancer and a striptease artist, but she wants to make a new life for herself, which happens to include that she's H.I.V. positive. We all know what that means. But, so far so good.

I've accepted her as my partner and, hopefully, together we'll find a way to throttle that disease." Then, "Now you know where we stand on this issue, too, but please, no pity. We know where your hearts are."

Nobody wanted to leave the party, as this incident seemed to have bonded them more closely together. There were at least twenty invitations for Sonja to individual homes to get to know her better. It was dark when the last cars finally drove off, leaving a very happy couple behind.

The next day, however, Dennis Blackwell phoned, and he had to have the last word in getting his point across, so he said, stressing every word, "I was not drunk yesterday, Phil, as you inclined; I was dead sober."

Also stressing every word, Phil replied, "We made our choices yesterday, Dennis; there is no more to say."

"You're living behind the times," Dennis came back; "I feel sorry for you guys." And that ended the caller's short conversation, unfortunately, on a very bitter note.

Philip looked at Sonja, and he couldn't even laugh. "He won't be back at our next year's party, and he knows it, too."

* * *

Late in the afternoon, Sergeant Whetherby was on the phone: "You might be interested in learning this, Phil, the goat has been adopted by the two high school girls. They wanted to let you know because you mentioned to them being worried about it. It's just been channeled in, if I may call it that."

"I'm sure glad to hear that," Phil replied; "the poor thing looked rather shaggy. It could use some human care."

"The other thing might be of great interest to Sonja," Will continued. "Two of our policemen's wives, having been policewomen themselves at one time, are running a party, kind of for terminally ill woman. It's actually a camp in the wild and it includes climbing up rock faces, roping across a river, among other very difficult feats. It might be helpful to get up their self-esteem again and to have courage to face whatever comes."

Phil said, "What a wonderful idea; of course, we'll accept. For a week, hey?"

Will replied, "I'll give you the address for the registration. It's in about two weeks."

"Thanks, Will, thanks a lot," Phil ended the conversation.

But he had not expected his mate's reaction. "You just accepted for me, and what do I have to say, sir?"

Phil felt anger creeping into Sonja's persona, as he tried to simmer her down. 'Did I take my responsibility for her for granted?' he wondered, then out loud he said, "It will do you good, girl. They all are women and all are very sick."

"Well, I'm not sick yet," she countered. "And you said yes for me, without even looking at me."

"Oh, Sonja, you're afraid in your deepest inner self, that's what it is," he said calmly. "You don't have to go, you know."

"And how would I look," she shot back, "after you accepted already?"

Phil thought, 'That's anchored fear in her subconscious mind, and she hates to see it come to the surface. She doesn't want to admit, not even to her inner self, that she, too, is terminally ill, and she's fighting it all the way. I'd better keep quiet and let her work it out on her own; no use arguing, in the state she's in. I'd better calm her down first.' Then said, "I apologize, if I did the wrong thing, Sonja." He got up and walked outside into the sun, lying down on one of the porch chairs and closing his eyes to contemplate.

It might've been half an hour, when Phil felt Sonja's present. She knelt down on a pillow and, bending over him, he felt her tears dripping onto his skin. He took her head and rested it down on his chest, where she sobbed and sobbed. Finally then, wiping her tears and looking into his eyes, she said quietly, but with determination, "I'm not terminally ill yet, Phil."

"I know that, of course, but you have to learn to face that possibility, my dearest one. Let go of your deep inner fear, because that's really bound to bring it about." He put his fingers through her hair. "You must stop feeling sorry for yourself. Besides, that camp could do you a lot of good, physically. You can use it on all levels of endeavor." This was followed by more sobbing.

Three weeks later, Phil heard the house door being unlocked, and it only could've been Sonja, back from the camp in the wilderness. He rushed to the door to receive her, anxious to hear what she had to report. Dropping the bags, she put her arms around him, obviously glad to be home again, then, in tears, she said, "At least I'm back with you again. It was not quite what I expected, but it did do me a lot of good."

Because it was a cool day, Phil had the fireplace crackling, and that's where they seated themselves. She began, "I was the only one, where the death threat was not yet evident, but I learned a lot from all the other women and made many friends. After I had revealed your life's philosophy of reincarnation and the law of cause and effect, they all wanted to know more, and some of them were really anxious. Not knowing too much myself, I gave them the titles of the books you had given me."

"You did well," Phil said, patting her hand, "one has to be careful and discriminating in this business, so let them do their own research. We'll help with more information, when asked."

A bit later he said, "So, they really taught you some discipline there, how to look after yourself and be strong in character?"

"How else could we've climbed up that cliff, Phil?" Sonja asked, "it sure taught me to have courage, you can believe that."

"Yes, yes, of course," her mate agreed, enjoying her enthusiastic explanation.

Chapter 5

Moppy's Last Mission

"I see your pistol licence has come in," Phil said as he leafed through the mail, having just come from a shopping trip. "From now on you can wear it, and I will let you know when."

Sonja showed him the paper and said, "I guess I have to have this with me also all the time."

Surprised, Phil said, "I see your second name is Alexandra; mine is Alexander. My dad often called me Alexander The Great, to my disliking. With that he meant to implant in me the idea to really become a great person some day. We never were close, and mother drank herself to death. When I came home from the war, I packed up my few belongings and went straight out west. I never saw him again, as he died soon after."

"I ran away when I was sixteen," Sonja explained. "I simply could not stand my parents' fanatical Jewish belief. So I left Edmonton and also came out west, to take the exact opposite path, which wasn't right either, of course. And now I have to put up with AIDS..." and she trailed off.

"I still maintain that you should visit that doctor in Los Angeles. His success stories are undeniable, and most of his patients are terminal cases. Your AIDS will not go away all by itself; why not do something about it now, while you're still physically fit?"

Sonja reluctantly answered, "Well, maybe I should, not that I like the idea too much. One has to be convinced of something, Phil."

Feeling her resistance, he didn't pursue it. At that moment the phone rang, "Is this 2999 Adler Street, Detective Wilbock?"

"You've got him," Phil replied.

A man's voice spoke again: "The police gave us a tip on you. Our bank is missing a substantial sum of money, since several million dollars were transferred two days ago. It points to mismanagement on our side, but I believe that the money has been stolen. We, including the police, looked at every possible avenue, but nothing. However, the sum of eight hundred thousand is missing, and there are no bones about it. Will you investigate, please? We might've overlooked something. We prefer it to be done without the public eye on us, in private. We'll pay you well."

"How about meeting me in my car," Phil suggested, "and then you tell me more about it."

The bank's president had invited Phil for lunch to a small restaurant, and that include Sonja. Apparently, four men in an armored truck had picked up nine million dollars of paper money, packed in several large bags, and then brought it from the bank here to another part of the city, where the bank had a large vault. It was all photographically recorded, so there couldn't have been any slip-ups, yet one bag with $800,000 was missing.

Several times they drove past the bank, later on, with the bank president explaining how it was handled. The armored truck waited outside and, while two men stayed inside the vehicle, the other two made several trips back and forth with the bags. There were four additional guards with shotguns, protecting the whole operation, with movie cameras along the way, recording every phase.

When they parted, Phil said, "It looks ticklish, all right, but I will try to put more light onto the situation. Give me a few days, please."

Inside the car, and on their own again, Phil said, "I

think I will call on my old friend, Welda Eisen; her little dog might be of help. That little animals has an unbelievable nose and she has the uncanny ability to smell out paper money. By the way, Welda is also a Jew; you met her at the party."

Dialing on the car phone, he called her and she answered at once, then invited them for afternoon tea.

They hugged at the door and she led them into, what she called her 'visiting parlor', then said, "Good Moppy is getting old now, Phil, but her nose is still intact. If you only knew, young lady, how many cases my Moppy has solved on the leash of that famous detective...." She pointed with a dry grin toward Philip. "I have it all recorded here in this journal and hope to publish it some day, after Moppy is gone."

And so, while slowly sipping their tea, some of the most intriguing stories were told by the hostess, who prided herself on being one of Phil's best friends, and to be able to loan him her smart little dog to 'deter the criminal elements of this big city,' as she put it.

"Hey, let's dine out tonight," Phil suggested to Sonja. "I know a restaurant where they allow dogs, and we will have a special treat for her, too."

It was almost dark, when they finally came to the bank building and, after letting Moppy sniff some paper money, they walked the outside route the men had taken with the bags toward the armored truck. Phil did it several times, and the dog always stopped at the sidewalk where the vehicle had been parked.

"I don't understand it," he said, "the truck itself is clean. My intuition is telling me, however, that some foul play happened before they loaded the bags, but how? It's all recorded by the cameras."

Then he knelt down on the sidewalk and shined his penlight on some cracks. "You see here? They use slates and this particular one is rather large and exactly square. See that? I need my magnifying glass. Tomorrow at daylight we'll be back. We might find a clue here, I feel." Before they left, he stomped his foot on the large slate, to see if it sounded hollow.

As they were driving again, Sonja said with a grin, "I

see some bushes there, near the railroad tracks. I wouldn't mind a quick sitting, Phil, as mother nature is rather pressuring me."

Phil said, "That will give me a chance to take Moppy on a little run, as she likes this kind of environment."

Five minutes might've gone by and Phil called out, "Hey, Sonja, we're here girl. Where are you?"

Getting no answer, he suddenly became very concerned and called out again: "Sonja? Sonja!"

Then, after having taken the dog off the leash, he said, "Something is very fishy here, Moppy, come on, look for her!" And they began penetrating the dense bushes, accompanied by loud barking.

Moppy ran and suddenly began to bark even louder. Following on the run, Phil came upon a bent-over figure and, drawing his pistol, shouted, "Get up or I'll shoot!" He kicked the man in the side, then he saw Sonja under his hands. This time Phil kicked him much harder, but the man hardly moved.

A shot rang out, as Phil aimed at his arm, and again shouted, "Let go of her!"

Of a rather heavy stature, the man began to scream and holler, holding his arm. Phil pushed him over with all his might to get at Sonja. She had a thin rope wrapped around her neck and suddenly a shrill shriek left her throat. "By god, she's still breathing!" Phil exclaimed.

At that moment, the detective saw a movement out of the corner of one eye; the criminal was taking a swing at him, but only brushed his head lightly. This time Phil kicked the man in the genitals with all the force he could muster, and it caused a terrible roar, similar to that of a wild animal.

Fortunately, Sonja was breathing deeply now, and she staggered to her feet. Feeling around her neck, she said with a trembling voice, "I'm okay, Phil; don't worry about me."

But he noticed that she was shaking all over, so he started to put his arms around her, then, unbelievably, the criminal was raising a gun at them. Pushing his mate aside, the detective was quicker, though, and his pistol shot was deadly accurate; dropping both the weapon and the man to the ground.

In spite of this, Sonja recuperated quickly and said, “I feel fine now, Phil.”

Loosening their embrace, Phil raised her jacket and called out in surprise, “Hey, your holster is empty, where is your gun? I asked you to carry it.”

“I left it in the car,” she answered meekly, feeling rather guilty.

“Do you understand that you almost got us both killed?” he asked in a loud tone. “Your negligence nearly cost us our lives. Oh, girl, and I thought at camp they finally funneled some discipline into you. Don’t you see how important that is in our business? In fact, in any business, like your AIDS, for instance.”

“I’m very sorry, Phil,” she apologized. “What else can I say?”

“Your apology is accepted, of course,” he said, quieter now, “but remember, when you’re dead it doesn’t do much good.”

“I’d better keep an eye on this creature, while you phone the police now,” he suggested.

Much later, already after midnight, Phil and Sonja entered the house and she still was rubbing her neck. “Let me have a look at it,” he said. “Well, you will have an unnatural blue ring around your neck for a while, a good reminder…” He didn’t finish the sentence.

After Sonja had gone to bed, Phil took Moppy on his arm and said, “You saved our lives and I thank you with all my heart.” The animal’s tongue found it’s mark.

Next morning at breakfast, Phil said, “You must know by now that I’m not angry, because anger never solves anything. However, I had to make a point with my words last night and I don’t know how else I could do that. I think it best you stay ‘off the beat’ for a while. Reflect in earnest on what happened last night, please?”

After Philip had left, Sonja drove to her own apartment. She knew now that she had to take stock, and also realized that love was not an everything heal-all ingredient in their relationship. It was only too true, of course, that her negligence had jeopardized their lives.

"Discipline," she said out loud, "if I cannot acquire discipline, once and for all, and anchor into my being after this terrible happening, I never will have it. He's right! He's right!"

* * *

In the meantime, Phil, now equipped with his detective bag, was on the prowl again near the bank, with Moppy tagging along. He parked the car right in the back of the building, where the armored truck also had been parked at the time, and behind the vehicle he bent down, as inconspicuous to any passer-by as he could be, to examine the large slate again with his magnifying glass. It seemed that the grooves bordering the surrounding slates were not very tight; the mortar was partly missing.

Then he took his little hammer, to knock on all the slates and found that the big one sounded different, if not hollow. Then Moppy put her nose down and tried to scratch with one of her front paws. "You think we might have something here, old girl? It's a possibility, you know." He patted the little dog.

Phil thought, 'This very spot is in a dead spot for all of the cameras, so, somebody could've slipped the bag quickly under the slate. However, I won't lift it up now and cause all kinds of commotion; we have to catch the perpetrators in the act.'

Later he advised the bank president to have at once a hidden infrared camera installed with a 24-hour view of that very same spot on the sidewalk. "It's a hunch," he said.

He hardly had entered his house, when the phone rang. "Boy, you're hard to reach, Phil." It was Sergeant Whetherby. "You know who you caught last night?"

"Gee, Will, nothing comes to mind," Phil replied.

"The notorious 'park butcher'!" Will called out.

"But that criminal hasn't been heard from for years," Phil voiced his surprise.

"You just wait until you hear the whole story." And so the astonished detective listened and listened, then realized that he indeed had captured a human killing machine, who, for years, was able to fool the police – they didn't even know who he was.

For eight years this criminal had killed almost forty, predominantly young women and girls, mainly prostitutes, until four years previous, when the killings suddenly stopped. At that time he moved to Chicago, where he then lived with his sister. There he continued his terrible business until a month or so back, when his sister became aware of her brother's murderous activities. So he ended her life before she was able to inform the police.

"Your shots didn't do him in, Phil, as he's like a bull and needs something stronger. We have this creature in continuous shackles at the hospital, and he's not getting out of our grip, you can bet on that."

Phil reflected, "It all sounds so strange and unbelievable, and, to think of it, a little dog actually prevented two more murders added to his list."

"Yes, I heard the whole story," the sergeant commented. "How is Sonja doing? You weren't too hard on her, Phil?"

"I gave her hell and a good verbal lashing," Phil answered. Then he added with a mellower voice, "Well, not quite. What would you've done, old boy. Both of our lives were on the line. If it wasn't for Mrs. Eisen's Moppy, we would've had it. No Will, I said what I had to say and she'd better learn about discipline, or ..."

The sarge interrupted him with, "She's still young, Phil –"

"Yes, yes, yes..." Phil stopped himself. "Look, I'm not angry, but she has to learn a lesson; any better way you know? Let her do some thinking. She's at her own place right now, perhaps some of the policemen's wives can have a chat with her."

* * *

"How did you possibly know that the bag of money might've been stowed under the sidewalk?" the bank president asked Phil, calling on the phone.

"Oh, it was more of a hunch than anything else," the satisfied detective replied. "Besides, that particular section of the sidewalk was not in view of any of your cameras."

"Three days after we had the infrared camera installed," the president explained with a jubilant voice, "the two men who thought out this criminal feat, emerged during the early morning hours, to collect the bag of money. They were two of the armored truck people. How can we thank you, Mister Wilbock? You sure did this bank a big favor."

"Having solved the hoist mystery," Phil said dryly, "was satisfaction to me more than any financial rewards."

"The financial rewards will be quite substantial, too," was the reply. "Our board of directors had put up ten thousand dollars to solve this case. Naturally, that goes to you."

With this news Phil could not really be happy, as he was thinking about Sonja. 'I'd better phone her right now,' he thought, 'and see what she's doing.'

"I knew it was you, Phil, when the phone rang."

In his quiet tone he said, "I wanted to tell you that my love is undiminished."

"I know that," was her simple answer. Then, a bit more lively, "I had at least half a dozen visits from policemen's wives and one of Sergeant Whetherby's aunts, who has throat cancer. We two will go to Los Angeles to see this doctor. I would've gone on my own, Phil, as my mind was already made up."

"Hey, you need somebody to drive you to the airport?" Phil offered.

"That would be great," was her eager reply, then, a moment later she said rather quietly and slowly, "You know, Alexander, I have been very stupid and am deeply ashamed of that, ashamed of all my holdouts. I call you by your second name, Alexander, because you're really the greatest."

"No, my dearest, there are much greater elements," Phil replied, "and we're surrounded by them every day, every minute; they will help us, if we let them. I'm only one of their instruments."

A moment later, he said, "By the way, good old Moppy died the other day. Her last job was to save particularly your life."

"Oh, Phil, I have to cry … what a noble and truly loyal animal."

"Now she's visiting me in my dreams," Phil explained, "and licking my face. Where do I ever find an equal replacement."

* * *

Philip Wilbock came home late, having been on a very tiring divorce case, and, to his utter surprise, Sonja's car was parked on the side of the driveway. He rushed in through the garage door and found his mate in the kitchen, smiling and anxiously awaiting him. They embraced without words and held on for a long time. With tears in her eyes, she finally said, "Well, Alexander, now you've got an Alexandra facing you. Hopefully, you'll understand the meaning of it?"

"Oh yes, my dearest girl," he sighed, looking deeply into her eyes, "I do grasp the significance of it, but tell me more, tell me more."

"You wouldn't believe what that doctor does, Phil, by simply turning on love, real love. And he does it with the employment of discipline, can you believe that?"

"Yes, I can. I knew that for a long time." He patted her on the arm.

"By turning on their love, so called 'given up' terminal cases are healed," she explained with emphasis. "Learn to love thyself first, was his motto, then love thy fellow men. I've learned so much, so much. And Sergeant Whetherby's aunt was even more enthusiastic than I. She's staying for another few weeks." A moment later, she followed it with the words, "I wonder how many people are willing to believe this kind of thing? Not many."

"How many people are willing to believe in anything invisible?" Phil mused, "wether it's intuition, spirit or the simple power of love? How many of us take the initiative and ask their assistance in our everyday life? But we pray often, and then expect their help to fall in our lap, never lifting a finger."

For a late sitting in the hot-tub, Sonja concluded, "Now I'm quite sure that my AIDS will soon be part of the past, Phil, if you can believe that."

Naturally, those words made Philip's heart and soul jump with joy.

Chapter 6

The Simulated Schizophrenia

As they were driving through the city, Sonja said to Philip, "I wonder whether we could pass by the place where that criminal almost strangled me to death. That incident changed my whole life; it really woke me up."

Phil nodded and changed direction. "Yes, I can see your point. Besides, it is excellent psychotherapy, when a person's life was endangered and other drastic happenings occurred, to visit that very same spot again, often only for the sake of peace of mind."

Having parked the car, they wandered along the bushes toward the railroad tracks. Finding a trail, they slowly walked through the wild growth. "We could have a picnic here … it's actually a nice spot."

"Yes, let's get some sandwiches," Sonja agreed.

As they strolled back to the car, a wild-looking dog watched them from afar, but seemed afraid to come near, in spite of their friendly calling.

Twenty minutes later, and having found a log to sit on, the two enjoyed their outing and the food in the fresh air.

Suddenly the very same dog they had seen before, approached them from behind, so they offered it bits of their sandwiches. "That little thing is half starved to death," Phil observed; "look at his ribs sticking out. He can have the rest of my bread."

"Mine, too; I still have the salad," Sonja offered with compassion. "Look at him gulping it down."

By now the dog had come so close they were able to stroke and pet the poor looking animal, then it crouched down right in between them.

"I wonder..." Phil began. "He certainly does not belong to anybody. You think we should take him to the SPCA?"

"Yes, let's," his mate agreed enthusiastically; "he sure needs more than we can give him."

They had no trouble getting the little creature into the car. While driving, Phil suddenly had an idea. "Hey, let's phone Welda Eisen; perhaps she will look after him, and give him a bath first."

Phil phoned his old friend on the car phone. "Hi, Welda. You wouldn't believe this, but we found a badly neglected doggy, right at the very same spot where Moppy did her last noble job, and we were on our way to the SPCA, but then thought about you. But ... perhaps you don't want another one –"

"Of course, I want another one," she interrupted, "but where do you find one like Moppy."

"Well –" Phil began.

"Bring him here," she interrupted him again; "maybe he is the reincarnation of Moppy."

When Welda saw the dog, she instantly took him into her arms. "It's a male though," Phil said.

"What do I care," his friend huffed, looking at him with surprise. "Can't you see the Moppy in him? So, now she's a boy. Oh, Phil, it's all been arranged by God, and you were his instrument, as you were so often with Moppy." Then she said to Sonja, "Yes, young lady, spiritual history is being made here."

They left a very happy Welda Eisen, and Sonja couldn't hold on until she asked, "Is that really possible, Phil? I mean, do dogs reincarnate too?"

"Perhaps even faster than we humans do," he replied.

* * *

There had been a telephone call from San Diego; a woman wanted Phil to call her back. When he got her on the line, she explained that her half-brother, a physician, suddenly had stopped writing, and she said, "He is a highly intelligent and loving man, and he wouldn't do this unless, of course, he died. But I can't pay much."

Phil said to Sonja, "That might be a simple case; often relatives are over-anxious and blow things out of proportion. We'll see...." Then, "I want you to stay here and take some possible calls. I'll probably be back in an hour or so."

Phil left and headed for a large hospital, where the doctor had done important research, and there he asked where he could find out more about Dr. Menser. He was directed to the office of Dr. Heinreich, the head of the whole conglomerate. "I didn't even know he had a sister in the States," he told the detective. "Unfortunately, Dr. Menser has developed slowly into a very bad case of schizophrenia. At times, highly intelligent people are only a hairbreadth from mental disorder. Well, this is not a mental disorder, per se, but rather a short-circuiting of some brain cells and no cure has been developed as yet. He has a brilliant mind, but this mental disease finally took hold of him. I have him under continuous sedation now because of the terrible pain he's under."

"Can I see him?" Phil asked.

"Of course, come with me, please." The doctor led the way to the ninth floor of the hospital, where only the severe mental cases were located, Phil was informed. "Because of Dr. Menser's extensive work with us, we have him in a room all by himself; he deserves good treatment, even now, until the end. What would I give to bring him around again."

Phil saw a slumbering man in the bed, jerking once in a while, caused by brain shock, as the doctor explained. The detective asked, "Can I visit him at times, to give his sister a report on his state, until he passes away?"

"If you give me her address, I'll send her a report on how her brother, very dear to me, fell sick mentally, but is very well taken care of now. She can visit him anytime, of course," the doctor offered graciously.

Back in his car, Phil thought. 'This whole thing runs a bit too smooth, and this Dr. Heinreich also seems too smooth. In my profession a man of this nature is not easily trusted and my innards are giving me a warning.'

At home Phil said to Sonja, "We might have a case, but it'll be difficult to prove anything." Then he explained the entire situation to her.

Philip took a bunch of flowers to the patient the next day. The three male nurses on the floor were playing cards and, while asking them for a vase, they were wondering why he was bringing the poor doctor the flowers? Since he was not even aware of his surroundings."

"Well, his sister asked me to do that," Phil explained with a sadness in his voice. "She loves her brother dearly."

Before he walked down the corridor, he noticed them grinning behind their hands; there didn't seem any compassion in their makeup.

Phil had hardly entered the room and placed the flowers on the night table, when, to his utter surprise, Dr. Menser opened his eyes and whispered, "I'm drugged, will you help me?"

"Yes, of course," was his immediate answer.

"Here, take this cloth with capsules first and put them into your pocket," the doctor whispered with haste. "They're the drugs they feed me, but I brought them up again. They make me swallow them with a glass of water, to make sure I get them down." Then, "Look through the door first, please, as they check periodically, so be careful," he advised.

Phil looked through the slit of the door, but the nurses were not in sight; were still immersed in their card game, no doubt, all the way down the hallway.

"Doctor Heinreich is trying to get rid of me by simulating schizophrenia in my mind, and he almost was successful until a few weeks back, when the nurses neglected to give me the drugs. Then I began to realize what was going on and brought the capsules up again to prove later on...."

Phil interrupted him, "Yes, yes, I already suspected foul play, and that's why I'm back. You see, I am a detective, hired by your sister in San Diego. We've got to get you out of here soon, and I have a plan in my mind. Are you physically fit?"

"I'm very weak, but can walk slowly," was the reply.

"All right, all right, I can carry you part way down the stairs," Phil explained. Before he went on, he had a look through the door slit again, to make sure they would not be disturbed. Then he added in a more quiet voice, "Next to your room is the fire-escape, and the stairs lead all the way down into the basement garage, where we'll wait with a car. Tomorrow, I'll bring a workman's coverall for you to put on, so you won't look too obvious. It's ten floors down … you think you can make it?"

"I will give it my best try, although it seems like a long way down," the doctor remarked with pain in his voice.

"Don't worry, I'll carry you. I'm used to leg work." Phil sounded encouraging.

Before he left, he had a few more words with the three male nurses. "Poor fellow; what can one only do to please his sister?"

"Nothing," was their unified answer.

In the basement parking lot, Phil quickly located the fire-escape door, opened it and went all the way to the ninth floor, to make sure that the door there could be opened. He had to bring a thin, but strong piece of plastic, to keep the door from snapping closed again, since it couldn't be opened from the inside. But, just in case, he intended to bring a bunch of his detective keys along, if an emergency should arise.

Coming home, Phil explained the whole situation to Sonja and excitedly said, "This action all by itself makes it worthwhile to be in this occupation." Then he laid out a plan: "We both drive into the underground garage and park as closely as possible next to the fire-escape door. We'll put a few blankets into your car's trunk, because that's where the poor doctor will be placed. No use to cause any suspicion when you drive out again. And then you take him to <u>your</u> place, where you prepare a temporary home for him. The reason for this might come to light later perhaps. In the meantime, I'll go up to the ninth floor again with the elevator, as if nothing happened. I'd like to see their faces when they discover his absence."

The next day it all worked out as discussed, until Phil came to the ninth floor, where he heard a loud commotion coming out of Dr. Menser's room. He quickly made up his mind to leave the workman's coverall – the clothing he had brought for the doctor to wear – behind the fire-escape door, but to keep it from snapping closed with the plastic piece he had brought along for that purpose. Then he entered the doctor's room, pretending he had come up the elevator.

Two of the male nurses had just tightened down the poor doctor. "He tried to walk around," one of them explained. "We can't have that. Maybe you can calm him down." Then they left.

"I'm sorry," the doctor whispered, "I got too excited and left the bed already."

"I could take you out right now," Phil said, "but then they'd know, for sure, that I did it. So, we will have to go through the whole process again. I'll leave by the elevator and come back via the fire-escape, where the coverall is waiting for you to put on. Don't worry, we'll get you out."

Ten minutes later, Phil was waving goodbye to the male nurses and said, with much sadness in his voice, "Poor man, death would do him good."

After a few quick words to Sonja, he climbed the stairs to the ninth floor again. There everything was quiet and in three minutes he had untied the doctor. Then, with encouraging words, coaxed him through the fire-escape door to help him into the coveralls. From there it was more a case of carrying the feeble physician than using his own weak legs, all the way down to the basement.

Sticking his head through the door, got Sonja into action, and in no time, Dr. Menser was leaving the hospital inside the trunk of a car.

The wise detective decided against showing his face on the ninth floor again, as he thought, 'I might cause suspicion, having visited the patient only fifteen minutes before.'

* * *

The public never heard of Dr. Menser's escape until three weeks later. Dr. Heinreich tried very hard to get the patient back into his fold. With some justification, he suspected that the detective might've initiated the disappearance, so he had his house under surveillance by some hired strongmen. During this time – suspecting what was going on – Phil only left his house through one of the neighbor's yard and always wore a wig with long hair and sunglasses. There was no doubt anymore in his mind that they had tried to poison Dr. Menser to death, because he had been the real brains behind the research for a new medical discovery.

When Dr. Menser finally was strong enough again, he moved into his own apartment, to prepare himself to live a normal life anew, but also to expose his adversary. As the head of a large hospital and as a physician, Dr. Heinreich had almost caused his death, by means of declaring him a schizophrenic.

To stand by him, he had his sister come up from San Diego, then he called in the news media – what Philip surely thought would take much longer – to tell his story and expose Dr. Heinreich for his misuse of a physician's power and good ethics; he pointed to his own research and medical discoveries.

For days the papers were filled with this startling event and, of course, Dr. Heinreich denied any wrongdoing. To no avail he mounted a counterattack, but the evidence was too overwhelming.

During all this commotion, Phil, referring to the case being dragged into the public limelight, told Sonja, "I think I named it right when I put it into the category of intellectual rhetoric. I'm only too glad that we're left out of it, so far away."

After a week of this, Dr. Heinreich was found dead in his garage; he had committed suicide by inhaling carbon monoxide; putting the guilt squarely on himself.

With the police investigation completed, Sergeant Whetherby phone Phil and said, "Thanks to you, Dr. Menser had his life given back to him. However, I can't help it, my friend, there was more to all this. Perhaps some drug outfit got their 'foot in the door', but finally greed got the better of Dr. Heinreich. There's nothing in writing, of course, but too many open ends face our examinations, though."

"I was thinking along the very same lines, Will. There's too much going on in this direction today. By the way, Sonja and I are invited to Dr. Menser's tonight to an elaborate dinner; it's kind of a 'thank you' party, I suppose. I'm not particularly fond of this, but Sonja might enjoy it."

With several of his physician colleagues, friends and their wives present, the doctor paid honor to Phil, and, pointing to his guest, he said, "If it weren't for this man, I probably would've died, I simply was too weak to take my own initiative. Please join me by giving a toast and heartfelt thanks to Detective Wilbock." They all raised their glasses in his direction.

But Philip was not too happy with this attention, so he got up and said, "I cannot take this, without pointing to your sister, my dear doctor; if it hadn't been for her call to me, the bug surely would've gotten you in the ground." His remark caused everyone to laugh.

The detective then added, "I reacted on her request because that's my job. The rest was rather easy for us … we do that all the time."

With the attention shifted to the doctor's sister, Philip Wilbock began to relax, preferring to be the cause in his life, instead of the effect.

Chapter 7

"A Little Dog Like That..."

"Is this 2999 Adler Street?" a man's voice came over the phone.

Philip pointed to Sonja to answer. "Yes, this is 2999 Adler."

"Are you a detective or private investigator?" the man asked, giving the impression of being unsure, whether to ask for help or not.

"We do both," Sonja replied.

"Well, you see, my wife is bothered by somebody," the man explained. "At times he's following her and wants a date. But we're not sure ... it might be several men. We've grown tired of the voices on the phone and some shady figure following her when she's coming from the theater in the evening; she dances there occasionally. As a businessman, I'm not home all the time. Anyway, we don't think the police are interested because this probably goes on all the time. In any case, I found you in the telephone book under 'Investigators', and wanted to see if you can help us?"

Having received all kinds of personal information, hints and suggestions, pertaining to the would-be crank, Philip said to his mate, "This might be a long case and develop into a serious matter, or we might come across a mentally off-balance oddball."

A bit later, after they'd met the troubled couple, Philip suggested to his mate, "When she's going to the theater tonight to practice with the ballet, only a few blocks from their house, we'll follow her. We've told her not to take a car this time and, perhaps, somebody might show up. Tomorrow we'll install our own telephone answering machine at their place beside their own, and then have it going all the time."

* * *

It turned out to be much more complicated than Phil had anticipated. What he thought to be a crank in the beginning, was a very smart individual, who might even be a psychopath, but he was in no way stupid.

Fred and Millie Jacobie lived in one of the better and rich districts of the city, in a very large and comfortable home. Since Fred Jacobie – who had a degree in psychology, but did not work in this field – was often out of town, Phil had Sonja move in with the woman, and he suggested to his assistant, "This guy might be dangerous, so wear your revolver at all times and try not to show your face during the dark at the windows; let him think she's alone. We've got our special hook-up on the phone, so, when I'm close by, I can hear you. For a while I'll take the van and sleep in it near the house."

However, this went on for almost four weeks and they became lax because nothing happened. Particularly Phil longed to sleep in his own bed at home again. What they didn't know, though, was the very fact this stalker – still trying on the phone to get his subject, Mrs. Jacobie, to submit to his sexual lust – knew of Sonja's presence already. His calls from all over town, and even from long distance, very professionally changed voices. When Dr. Jacobie was at home, the calls always came in less and even stopped, raising questions and suspicions in Phil.

In a long conversation, Sonja revealed to Phil a lot of private and 'tender' relationships between the couple. Apparently sex was a very sophisticated art to him and he had his wife perform the darnedest acts of dance to get him into the right mood. Not that she was against it, but there were times when she was very tired and then told him to get it over with, which always upset him terribly.

This private insight put Phil's attention on a new possibility, that Dr. Jacobie could be in on this stalker's activities. Phil then thought, 'Not likely, but this man's telephone calls might arouse him sexually. Or could it be that he is a caller himself? I'd better put my eyes on that possibility.'

* * *

Meanwhile, Welda Eisen was finally able to reach her old friend. "Boy, you're a busy bee, Phil … for days I've tried to reach you."

"But why didn't you leave a message on the recorder?" he asked.

"No, Phil, this answering machine business never does appeal to me; I want you personally. Well, anyway, I think Tom has developed into a fine snoopy dog, and sometimes I even think he might be better than Moppy was at his age. I want you to try him out and see, if you have the time."

"So, you call him Tom?" Phil laughed. "Like Tom Sawyer in Mark Twain's novel?"

"Yes," she replied, "I always liked that adventurous boyhood story, and my Tom is like that; he's very smart."

Fifteen minutes later, Phil rang the bell at his friend's house, and, while they embraced, he said, "So we have another smart dog here." He hardly had the words out when Tom came running with a wagging tail toward the visitor, as if he recognized him.

"You see," Welda pointed out, "he still knows you, from the time you saved him. He has a wonderful memory, and his nose … I tell you, Phil, he's a miracle dog; even reads my thoughts at times. Oh, I'm so grateful you brought him to me; with other people he would've been completely lost, not understanding him."

This welcome information then gave Phil an idea. The night before, the detective had had a call from a group of parents; apparently their children at school, during their play and walks home, had been bothered by a man, who took a particular liking to the girls. They wanted to find this man and report him to the police, before anything serious might happen.

Phil thought, 'This might give me an opportunity to

try out Tom, if he just gets a sniff of the guy.' He hardly had entered his car, after having left his lady friend, when a woman of this group of parents called on the cellular phone. "Could you come over to the school, please, that man has been here again, just a short time ago."

"I'll be there in a few minutes," Phil satisfied her; "I was on my way anyway."

Walking to school, three eleven-year-olds had been talked to by this very same man. He wanted to give them candy and said that he liked them.

Arriving at the scene, Phil parked the car and got Tom's nose on the subject and, the way he was wagging his tail, he understood who they were looking for.

The anxious dog led them through a large park, along an abandoned railroad line, toward a part of the city with old houses, and then he stopped at the porch of one of them. The women wanted to enter the place and give this man a piece of their minds, but Phil stopped them. He was able to pull them back and said, "You've got to leave this to me, ladies, or we won't be able to catch this guy."

The detective was able to reach a police car on his cellular phone and they arrived there in three minutes flat. He knew one of the officers and, after having briefed them about the situation, suggested, "Let me ring the bell and talk to him first, while you stay out here in earshot range, hidden away."

A middle-aged man came to the door, and Phil said, "You have been bothering some kids at a school nearby; why are you doing that? Their parents are worried."

With a deep smile he answered, "But I don't mean any harm; I just like children."

Hearing that, the policemen came into view and, more serious now, the man said, "And you even called the police. I can assure you, I never would do any harm to them. I'm not one of those stalkers who takes them into the bushes."

After the irritated women exchanged some heated words with him, the police took him to headquarters, while Phil, the dog and the ladies walked back to the school. There, of course, they gave their satisfied report of having caught the culprit, thanks to Tom's nose. Everyone then started petting and patting the dog, to the delight of the little fellow.

And to Philip's deep satisfaction, Tom proved to be a top 'snoopy', as his lady friend, Welda Eisen, had named him.

* * *

The moment Phil entered his car next morning, Sonja called him: "You won't believe this, but Mrs. Jacobie has been raped right under our noses. While Dr. Jacobie worked in his office, and I was in the garden for a midnight stroll, somebody came through the open back porch door into her bedroom, where she was asleep at the time. Before she knew it, this masked man had gagged and bound her with tape, undressed himself shamelessly – can you imagine that, Phil? – and raped her as if he was her lover. I never heard anything about it, until this morning, after the doctor had left. First I thought she was kidding me, but when she began to cry, I had to believe her. The really repulsive thing to me though is that, after she had freed herself and ran to her husband in tears, he wanted to have sex with her, explaining that, from a psychologist's point of view, it would take the load of shame and guilt off her mind.

"I had wondered about a scream, coming from their bedroom, but only could hear their subdued voices through the door," Sonja continued. "This morning she appeared with tears and red eyes and told me the whole story with halting words. She's still terribly upset, so maybe you can have a few soothing words with her; you're so good at it, but I'm kind of lost."

"I have a funny feeling, Sonja, this case becomes more and more complicated, and we're not getting anywhere. We will have to take serious stock. I should be there in half an hour. Talk to you later."

On his drive to the Jacobie place, the detective thought, 'There seems to be something quite wrong with Doctor Jacobie and I'd better look deeper into his character. Could he be behind those telephone calls? I aim to find out, and the sooner the better. But, why in the world did he hire us? Something is awfully screwy."

As soon as Mrs. Jacobie saw the dog alongside Phil, she became very joyful and took Tom on he lap, affectionately stroking him. The presence of the animal seemed to have calmed her down.

After a while, Phil asked her, "I have to ask you, did you notice any mark or certain characteristics on this man? Some little detail...?"

"No, nothing," she replied. "He went about his business very physically with a grin on his face, like a ... like a charlatan. Yes, that's it, like a sure-footed charlatan. He gave me the feeling that he was a man of the world and everybody was his slave."

That short explanation anchored itself deeply into Phil's memory, as he knew this kind of a 'charlatan' when he saw one.

* * *

Equipped with several of the voices on tapes, who ever had tried to talk to Millie Jacobie on the phone in the lusty and greedy way, Phil called on an old doctor friend. After he had him on the line, he said, "Hi, Doc, long time, no see. Are you still in business?"

"Is that you, Phil? I thought so ... your voice I'll detect any time. No, I'm semi-retired and only work by referral. But, for you, my friend, the door is open day and night, particularly if you have a juicy case at hand."

"I have, I have," Phil said, then laughed. "Difficult, to say the least."

"I'm free, come on over. We can have a tea first," replied Dr. Albert Janersen.

When Phil arrived there, it was a hearty greeting at the door, indicating a mutual liking for each other.

"I see you've brought a little dog," the doctor said, pointing at the animal. "It's not Mrs. Eisen's Moppy, or is it?"

"No, my friend, it's Moppy's reincarnation, Tom." And over tea Phil told the whole story. "He already has proved himself. He's a very smart fellow, even picks up thoughts, as Welda Eisen tells me. He'll get plenty of opportunities with me, as you can imagine."

Some time later, after having explained the details of his present case, Phil said, "I brought here several tapes with all the voices who repeatedly call Mrs. Jacobie with odd, but mostly sexual, suggestions. With your help I'd like to establish whether they're all different people, or just one or two, trying to disguise the real caller. Listen to them, my friend, and tell me what you think."

Running the tapes repeatedly through the recorder, Dr. Janersen, an expert in voice identification, was listening intently. Finally he had made up his mind. "One, two, four and five are one and the same person. With three, I'm not sure, perhaps he is all by himself. Six and seven are also one person; he's a very clever man with a wonderful control of his voice."

Phil asked, "How does the word charlatan clock in your mind's computer, Doctor?"

"Yeah, yeah, that might hit the nail on the head," Dr. Janersen poked his forefinger to his chin, indicating recognition of a certain connection. "Yeah, I think charlatan fits the character of the man as well. He has no scruples whatsoever."

"I have another tape here, so tell me what you think about him?"

With the first part of the tape hardly played, Dr. Janersen excitedly called out, "That is the same man's voice on one, two, four and five!"

"Are you sure about that?" Phil asked again.

"No doubt, my friend, no doubt. From my point of view, this voice disguiser is not even clever. And he is the one who hired you? Beware of him; I don't know what his intentions might be. So far, however, he has fooled his wife and even you."

"I was wary of him right from the beginning," Phil replied. "My intuition was warning me."

"Yes, yes, of course, soul is the intuition," the doctor said with certainty. "It's God's voice and we'd better not ignore it."

Philip nodded with agreement.

* * *

Back in his car, the detective got a phone call from Sergeant Whetherby, "Gee, Phil, I wish we still had Mrs. Eisen's Moppy with us. There was a sex murder and our German Shepherd is kind of stuck."

"But, Will, we have a replacement. In fact, I have him with me right now. Where are you?"

"I'm on my way back to the office, but –"

"Make a U-turn and drive back to the scene," Phil interrupted him. "Where is it?"

"Near the theater, Phil. One of the ballet dancers was the victim."

In about five minutes the two friends shook hands and the sergeant said, while patting the dog, "Boy, he looks like good, old Moppy."

"Not quite, Will; he has her size, but Tom might even surpass her, we think. Come on, let's get at it, before the scent gets diluted and lost."

To the sergeant's amazement, Tom was at once all nose, as if he knew what to go after. They trailed the scent for over two blocks, where it stopped on the sidewalk. "Here that person entered a car. The important thing is, though, Tom has the smell recorded now," Phil explained, "and later on he will know it, I bet. He's a smart little dog, Will."

Phil paused, then said, "I'm on a case right now, protecting a woman who's being stalked by telephone, and she even was raped by this guy. She also works as a ballet dancer as a stand-by, and now I wonder whether there might be a connection. That guy is very clever, I tell you. I just came from Dr. Janersen, the voice expert, and he listened to this man. He says to watch out for him because he has no scruples. There's much more to this, of course; I'll let you know, Will.

"I'm kind of on the edge with this case, so I'd better get going, before another life is on the line," Phil concluded, then called the dog, "let's go, Tom."

* * *

Philip Wilbock was wondering how much of all he had learned from Dr. Janersen he should tell Sonja. Would she mentally and emotionally be strong enough to stay detached. Dr. Jacobie might feel her uneasiness when he comes home and take some action; after all, we know so little about him and his activities. Is he in some way connected with this sex murderer. His final thoughts were, 'I've got to work fast before another life is endangered, so I'd better leave my mate in the dark, partly anyway, as she's not an experienced detective, by a long shot, and might give us away.'

Coming to the Jacobie residence with a sandwich in hand, everything seemed quiet; the usual lights were on and nobody moved. So, he ate in peace, lost in thought, trying to manipulate all the faces and suspicions. He was very tired after the day's work, so he lowered his head for a nap, to join the dog in this endeavor.

Aroused again, he wiped his eyes and wanted to leave the car, when he saw Dr. Jacobie drive up to enter the garage. He recognized the detective's car and came over. "Trying to get hold of the stalker out here in the dark, hey?"

"No, not really," Phil replied, then smiled. "I simply fell asleep. The noise of your car woke me up."

"What have you got there beside you?" the doctor asked, "I didn't know you had a dog."

"I haven't. Good Tom here, with his fine nose, assists me at times." As soon as Phil had the words out, he regretted it, thinking, 'I should've left the doctor in the dark, and not reveal the dog's ability.'

"Are you coming in?" the doctor asked.

"Yes, I'd like a few words with my assistant." He locked his car.

The women were watching TV in the living room, but immediately turned their attention to Tom, who looked forward to their gentle hands with a wagging tail. The way the doctor greeted his wife seemed rather over-emotional, Phil observed, probably to give the detective a certain impression.

While the couple sat beside each other with a scattered conversation, Phil and Sonja went into the next room, where he briefed her on some of the day's events. But, suddenly there was a commotion in the living room, and Mrs. Jacobie cried: "The dog, the dog, it's in terrible agony."

Phil asked, "Did you give him something to eat?"

"Only a cookie," the doctor called out.

The detective's mind was racing for a few seconds about what to do, then he scooped up Tom and ran out of the house, calling back to Sonja: "I'll bring him to a doctor. You stay here." And out he went to the car.

Arriving at the closest hospital emergency entrance, he pleaded with the nurse and doctor, "There is no veterinarian nearby. I'm a detective, and it might be a matter of life and death." Nobody suspected that he meant his animal friend. "Please, pump his stomach out and preserve the contents, I have to know what kind of poison it is." To get them into action, he showed his identification.

They recognized the urgency and went to work. Miraculously, Tom came to life again and recognized his friend. Phil said to Tom, "I don't know whether you understand this, my beloved dog, but the man who gave you the cookie is evil and we're going to get him."

When Phil wanted to pay, they looked at each other and then waved him off, to forget it. One of the doctors said with a smile, "In this hospital, only humans pay."

Very grateful to them, Philip gave them his card, "If you ever need help…" and he shook their hands.

With the bottle of the dog's stomach contents in his pocket, Phil carried Tom outside and when he entered the car, said, "We're going to a safe home now, my devoted friend, for you to recuperate." On the advice of one of the doctors, the dog lapped up a dish of milk to neutralize his stomach again.

Next day it was established that Tom had been given straight rat poison. That fact put the detective into a bind, more or less. 'What is that Jacobie guy trying to do?' he asked himself. 'Giving this poison to the dog was simply too obvious; he knows I'm not stupid. He wants to give me a warning, of a sort, either or even to get me and Sonja out of there. But why did he hire us in the first place? To have an alibi later on, perhaps, on some of his activities? He must know that a detective is not born yesterday and might even be able to discover his schemes, whatever they might be. Drugs!' several times that word popped into Phil's mind, as intuition. 'From now on I shall concentrate on his activities, they could give me the answers I'm looking for.'

A moment later, his thoughts went over to his mate.

'I'd better have a good talk with my beloved Sonja. Hopefully she recognized the poisoning of the dog as a warning last night. No, I doubt she suspected anything. I'd better bring Tom back to Welda, so she can pamper him a bit.'

* * *

The detective in Philip Wilbock was working hard. 'What should he say when facing Dr. Jacobie?' he wondered. 'I'm quite sure by now that he knows that I know. Should we continue our game of pretenses?'

Arriving at the doctor's house, however, relieved him of any immediate decision; it was taken off his consciousness because Dr. Jacobie had left early in the morning for a long business trip. He couldn't help thinking, 'Why is he keeping Sonja and me on? Even paying us a good amount of money. Surely not only to protect his wife. The more I work for this man, the less I like it. He's using us somehow, and I'd better get a handle on what it is?'

First of all, the women wanted to know about Tom, was he all right? "He's doing rather well," Phil reported, not wanting to reveal what really happened. "I've brought him back to Mrs. Eisen, his home. We like each other, but he feels better there." And he winked to Sonja not to pursue it.

Then, with tears running down her cheeks, Millie Jacobie mentioned that she had known the murdered ballet dancer well; in fact, they had been friends at the theater. Only her husband's attitude had prevented them from having a closer relationship at their home here.

Now the detective was all ears, and he thought, 'Could there be a connection? Could the rape murder of the ballet dancer and the rape of Mrs. Jacobie be related? Could it be the very same man?'

Before he left the women and with Sonja alone, he urged her to be very careful and never leave Mrs. Jacobie out of sight. Parting from her at the front door, he said, "I suspect that this criminal is very dangerous and next time he might kill your ward. And no matter what you do: toilet, kitchen, bedroom, or the rest of the house, keep the pistol on you."

She embraced him and said with trembling words, "I will try to talk to you on the phone several times a day. Oh, Phil, I'm afraid, but I will do my job."

It was easy for the detective to find the taxi-cab that had brought Dr. Jacobie to the airport early, and the driver reported that Dr. Jacobie always was brought to a private departure terminal at the airport.

Phil further discovered that only one private jet had left early, toward South America.Then he said to himself with displeasure, 'I should've followed this lead from the beginning. However, now things are brightening up. I bet he's into the drug trade, and I'd better give my friend, Sergeant Whetherby, a run-down on this man.'

* * *

Two weeks had passed and nothing out of the ordinary happened, concerning Mrs. Jacobie and her husband, but Phil cautioned Sonja. "Don't become too lax, please; out of experience I know that things always seem to come back to you when least expected."

That was during a morning visit to the Jacobie place. In the late afternoon the detective had an urgent telephone call from his assistant, and her voice sounded loud and hoarse: "Phil, Phil! I shot that guy, while he wanted to grab Mrs. Jacobie. I warned him, but he came toward us, so I pulled the trigger. He turned and escaped; his blood is all over."

With thoughts working overtime, he quickly phoned Sergeant Whetherby, explaining the situation. Then he drove to Welda Eisen to pick up Tom, the dog. He left her in a rush, calling back, "Big things are in the making, Welda, see you."

The police were already there when Phil arrived at the Jacobie house. Immediately he put the dog on the attacker's tail, whose blood still was visible a block away, Excited, Tom followed the scent for five blocks to the theater and two blocks past that, where it stopped. No doubt, here he had entered his car again, the very same spot as that of the rape murder. "He's one and the same," Phil said to the dog.

His intuition told him to continue walking in the same direction the car had been pointed, hoping that the dog might pick up a scent once more, not too far away. And his hunch was right!

Four blocks away, Tom suddenly let out an excited howl and put his nose to the bottom of a closed garage door. "We got him," Phil whispered, "just sit tight."

"Hey, Will," Phil said with a subdued voice on the cellular phone he carried in his pocket, "Have you an inkling where Tom and I are standing right now?"

"You found the guy!" his friend called out.

"Yes, and we're standing in front of his garage," the detective said, leaving no doubt. "He is the one Sonja shot and also the rape murderer. As I suspected, they're one and the same. You'd better send a squad car to this address, and warn them that he might be dangerous."

"I'll come myself, Phil, hang on." And he quickly was off the line.

Sergeant Whetherby came with two police cars and they surrounded the house without much noise, to the surprise of the neighbors. When the knock on the door didn't bring any results, they broke it down and found the profusely bleeding suspect in agony on his bed. He was a slender, black-haired white man, as described by Mrs. Jacobie and Sonja earlier, and not Dr. Jacobie, of course, who had been suspected by the sarge at one time.

Later on, while searching the house, all kinds of material was found, indicating the man's abnormal sex desires and lifestyle. Apparently, he found only real satisfaction while raping his victims and then choking them to death. He could be classed a psychopath.

Riding together to the Jacobie residence, the sergeant was telling his friend with satisfaction, "Boy, what a haul this was, thanks to Tom's fine nose. I'm not trying to belittle your detective abilities, though, Mr. Wilbock...." He laughed, "but..."

"I don't mind at all, Will;" he interrupted him, also with a laugh. "The spotlight never suited me anyway. If Tom here gets it, that's okay with me." They both laughed, while Phil stroked the dog with delight.

"I'm so glad you got him finally," Mrs. Jacobie greeted the two men, as they entered the living room, where the police still were taking blood samples. "Now I can relax again."

Phil laughed to himself and thought, 'You don't know the husband you have, or, perhaps, you don't want to know.'

Then Sonja asked, "How did he get into the house? Everything was locked. He seemed to know where we were. It's a puzzle to me."

"I bet he was inside the house already for a while, observing the situation," Phil suggested. "Probably watching from upstairs. Hey, I have an idea … let our good snoopy dog get his scent and see where he was."

To their surprise, the attacker had entered the premises from the upstairs balcony, which had a long row of stairs leading into the garden.

"But how did he open the balcony door?" Sonja asked. "It was locked tight."

Phil waved his index finger slowly through the air, "I have a suspicion, but don't think I should table it here." And he glanced at Mrs. Jacobie.

Feeling somehow that it was concerning her and her husband, she quickly made up her mind with no regrets, and said, "I know it's about my husband. What you suspect, I felt deep down in my heart for quite some time, but was afraid to face it or admit to myself. I think that <u>he</u> gave the key to that man, perhaps to have me killed." There were no tears in her eyes.

As they walked downstairs again, Will whispered to his friend, "This is a police affair now, Phil, so you guys are relieved."

With a sudden idea, he whispered back, "Hey, Will, try to find the key from the balcony door on that guy, and perhaps you can squeeze out of him that he got it from Dr. Jacobie."

The sergeant grabbed his friend's arm with delight, seeing daylight in these cases of rape and murder.

* * *

Three days after the rape intruder had been shot and caught, Phil got an urgent call from his police friend late in the afternoon, "Lieutenant Little George from the waterfront division just called me, and they have a large container ship there and he suspects that it has cocaine aboard. He tells me that some of those containers probably are loaded with the stuff, because every time this ship comes to Vancouver, the streets are flooded with the drug. Their dog can't sniff out anything and they cannot take all the containers apart without proof. At once I thought about Tom, Mrs. Eisen's dog, and his fine nose, of course. The lieutenant told me that his intuition 'simply knocked on my conscience', to quote him, but without any kind of evidence, Phil –"

"We just happen to have Tom with us, Will, where do we go?"

"It's best you come here to headquarters first and then we take one of our cars," the sergeant suggested.

Half an hour later, they met the lieutenant, who couldn't help but remark, "You mean that little dog –? I hope you're serious."

"Simmer down, Henry," the sarge said very calmly. "That little dog just caught a rape murderer. We didn't think our German Shepherd could've done the job. In complicated cases we don't use them anymore. Now then, let's go to work. Tom here is itching already."

The lieutenant said, "I hate to unload the containers, but once ashore, we have to let them go."

"Are you trying to suggest that this little dog – any dog in fact – should run along all those stacked containers, Henry? Come on now … unload them, one by one, and Tom will find the booty, you'll see."

"I wish I had your confidence, Will, but what choice do I have." His look at the detective and his assistant wasn't very complimentary either.

Philip, who had been quiet, so far, said with a hidden grin, "Just give him a whiff of cocaine. You've got some handy, I hope."

There was no answer from the lieutenant, but his eyes showed contempt. He pulled out a little bag of cocaine for Tom to dig his nose into. Then he gave the signal to unload.

The first layers of eight containers showed absolutely nothing, from the viewpoint of the dog's smelling organ, and the waterfront policeman did not try to hide his scorn, as if he wanted to say, 'You and your dog!'

However, as the second layer of containers came

ashore, it began to happen: big, big, big! When the first container was sniffed out by Tom, the lieutenant's men went to work and in fifteen minutes had discovered six large bags of cocaine, all wrapped thickly in plastic.

As the dog indicated another fifteen containers holding the very same 'precious' drug, Sergeant Whetherby suggested to Lieutenant Henry Little George, "I wager you, without having looked inside the containers, that they all have the same amount of that white stuff inside, if not more. How about a hundred bucks, Henry?"

With some embarrassment, he said, "I have to apologize. I was so helpless and my anger got the better of me, I'm afraid. That sure taught me a lesson. A little dog like that?" The lieutenant shook his head with amazement.

"You can have one too," Philip spoke up. "There's a woman right here in Vancouver who trains little dogs like this, but only one out of eight or so makes it. Tom here is a natural; he was born with his gifted nose."

"Yes," the sarge fell in, "he's the reincarnation of Moppy, who just died a few months ago. If you're willing to believe in that kind of thing." A grin toward Phil came over his lips.

"My Indian ancestors also believed in reincarnation for many centuries," the lieutenant explained. "Our old chief was the last who mentioned it. Now we have adopted the white man's religion."

Then Sonja asked with much enthusiasm, "From where do you think I know this man?" She grabbed Phil's arm. "Sure, in this life there're about forty years between us, but the love – from another lifetime – is still there." Phil gave her a hug.

Sergeant Whetherby felt kind of abashed, but became more at ease when the lieutenant said with a very serious face, "I believe you, young lady. I also want to apologize to you for being so rude in the beginning. This day has taught me more than all my other professional days together."

Philip suddenly asked, "By the way, were there not tourist cabins on this ship? Are the passengers all clean to go? I'm just curious; my intuition, you know."

"I don't think they're connected with this," the policeman said. "There's one, and he also rode with this boat, but he wasn't able to get a cabin."

"What's his name?" Phil and Will asked at the same time.

"Why? You don't think..." the lieutenant trailed off. "His name is Fred Jacobie."

Phil called out, while Will banged him on the back, "Hang onto him, lieutenant! He's probably the kingpin of this drug shipment. Besides, the police want him on an assisted rape and murder charge."

The joy of the two friends was boundless.

More serious then, Phil said, "As I know Dr. Jacobie, don't let him out of your sight. He knows by now, of course, that his drug shipment has been discovered. Do you have the other side of the ship under observation? He might try to escape from there, together with important data."

Quickly the waterfront police officer gave orders to have a man with a searchlight positioned on the wharf opposite the unloading side.

It was well after midnight when a man of the ship's crew jumped into the water, for whatever reason, but was apprehended a few minutes later.

At the very same time, a watertight bag, weighted down with heavy iron, had been tossed out of one of the portholes. However, it was brought back to the surface by a skindiver early in the morning.

That bag, as it was discovered some time later, was worth its weight in much more than gold, because it contained evidence of Dr. Jacobie's drug activities, namely that he truly was one of the drug operation's redundant kingpins.

Almost a billion dollars worth of cocaine was discovered in those containers, the largest haul in police history, at the west coast of Canada.

When the sarge phoned his friend in the morning, and after he had explained some of the previous day's details, he said, "It's good that we have Tom now, Phil, he's real. But reincarnation? Past lifetimes? I cannot lay my hands on that." He paused, then added, "I guess you're off to Mrs. Eisen's later on for a tea and another chapter to her dog journal. Sometimes I wish I wasn't in this uniform and could join you."

"Yes, now that you mention it. That will be our first relaxation in peace and quiet since how many weeks back? Almost two months."

"Hey, Phil," the sarge said, with some softness in his voice, "Sonja is developing into a real professional now. She was not afraid to face that guy and shoot him. Give her my regards, please."

"She's listening in, Will."

"Oh, is she? You did well, Sonja; my compliments." And he hung up.

Red-faced, she put her arms around her mate. "I was very much afraid, though, Phil."

"Oh, my beloved apprentice, under those tense circumstances we all are, you may believe that. Only the callous with no heart will shoot indiscriminately and make the wildest claims afterward of not being afraid. They have no place in our, or police, profession. In a way they're like criminals, without heart and soul, and the real meaning of love never was able to manifest in them."

In the closeness of her mate she found the validity of his words.

Chapter 8

"I'm Not in the Dark With This"

Philip Wilcock was dreaming, to find himself rolling down a long hill on a motorless scooter, with the fresh wind fanning around his face. Walking up the steep grade again, a boy approached him and asked, "Are you going to give me a ride?" He nodded, smiling.

A few moments later, Phil scooted down the hill again, with the joyful boy standing in front of him; only this time the downward journey went on and on and on. End of dream.

Sitting up in bed, he asked himself, "I wonder, what all that was about?"

Suddenly he remembered the face of the boy. It was Sonja's. "Maybe she was my brother then," he thought. "But what's the meaning of the scooter ride?"

At breakfast, later on, as he was trying to tell Sonja about the dream experience, she impulsively stood up and called out: "Hey, Phil, I was there, too!" Sitting down again, she followed it with the words, "Now I remember it. You took me on that scooter down the hill."

"You were a boy then," he grinned, "and my brother perhaps."

"I loved you then," she burst out, "I know I did! I felt it."

"All dreams are trying to tell us something," he explained. "Divine love does not care about gender, because soul is its origin and neither a he or a she."

Then, "I'm at a loss, though, over the long scooter ride with us two down the hill and its meaning."

"Maybe it means we two stay together forever...." She smiled at him.

"Even after death?" he asked. "Obviously, I'm the first to go. Perhaps as souls we never part, after all: soul is eternal."

* * *

Later that day, there was a call from a woman, who claimed that her husband had kidnapped one of her twin sons so Phil said to her, "That's a serious accusation, madam; wouldn't it be better to call the police and let them go after him?"

"No, no, he went to the States," she replied, "and our Canadian police have no power there. Besides, as you probably know, there's too much of this going on today here in Vancouver and they haven't got the time."

That sounded reasonable enough to the detective, so he and his assistant drove to the woman's place.

"I have to have all kinds of information, particularly about your husband," Phil said to Mrs. Audry Lee.

He had encouraged Sonja to get herself a little notebook and write things down. So, as Phil asked the questions, she recorded the answers, as she deemed necessary.

Her husband was Chinese and they had parted eight months previous. He had been back to see his newborn twin sons and asked to have one of them, which she refused. There was an older daughter, Angelica, seven years of age, who took it rather hard that her father would've done the kidnapping. Finally she said, "He's probably in San Francisco with his relatives, but I'm not sure of that."

In the attic there was a large trunk with some of his belongings and the detective would be back for fingerprints later on. He wondered, though, why the man hadn't taken the trunk with him, since they did not part in any rush.

Mrs. Lee also had an aged mother and several sisters and brothers. The oldest sister was in a hospital with mental disorders. "She was never quite right," the lady explained. “As children she often killed our pet animals, telling us younger ones that God loved them so much they had to go early. We had to put her away finally, it was too difficult to look after her.”

Gordon Lee had been in the Air Force, Phil discovered, while trying to find some leads and answers in his trunk. There was a large goblet, covered with his fingerprints. Out came his kit with brush and powder to take several samples. It was easy enough.

Mrs. Lee was very accommodating and even invited Phil to come back on the weekend while they visited the old mother.

However, in spite of all the positive information acquired and the help the lady tried to give to the detective, his insight was telling him that not all was as smooth as it appeared in this house, or with the mother whose baby had been kidnapped.

As they left the house, the seven-year-old daughter spoke to them in the hall and said, “Papa did not kidnap the baby; he would not do that because he loves us and he told mama.”

Without a wink, nor losing her temper, Mrs. Lee said, “But, darling, I know your father better than you do. He wanted one of the boys; you heard him say it.”

“He would not do that, mama,” the daughter objected; “he would not do that.”

This interchange of words between mother and daughter added to Phil’s suspicion, and during their drive home he said to Sonja, “Young children have a certain insight, and she might be right. I think we will try to find her husband, then we’ll know for sure whether the girl was right or not. In the morning we’ll be off to San Francisco.”

The Chinese community was a very large one in this big southern city at the west coast, and the name ‘Lee’ was quite common. “How do we find the right one, Phil?” Sonja asked her mate, while looking through the telephone book. “We can’t phone them all, and what do we say?”

“You’re right,” Phil replied in deep thought. “Let’s contemplate on this for a few moments, and perhaps some idea will manifest in our minds.”

Then, after having first inquired at the hotel desk, he said, “Every big city has a radio talk show, where one can phone in for information, or if one wants to help locating a friend or relative. Those hosts do everything under the sun to accommodate their listeners. So let’s write a few lines down he can put on the air, important in finding our Mr. Lee.”

Having their ears on that particular radio station, they heard twenty minutes later: “A Gordon Lee from Vancouver, Canada, is wanted. His wife’s name is Audry. Please phone this number at the Holiday Inn.”

In a considerably short time, the right Gordon Lee was on the phone, asking excitedly, “Did something happen to my wife or the children? Please tell me.”

“Nothing, Mr. Lee, nothing,” Phil tried to calm him down. “But we would like a talk with you. I could come to your place or meet you here at the hotel.”

They met a very gentle man in the lobby of the inn soon after, and Phil knew right there and then, that he never could’ve kidnapped one of the twin boys. And when he heard what his wife had accused him of, he said with some sadness in his voice, “That it should come to this … I had asked her to let me have the twins and my daughter occasionally, when the boys are older, of course. Now, she’s hiding one of them and blames me for the kidnapping. Who is it? Tyler?” Phil and Sonja nodded.

“I’m fairly well off,” Gordon Lee explained, “and her monthly check is rather large. I don’t understand what she tries to accomplish with this.”

When he heard then from the detective that is might not be a case of hiding the child, he offered himself to help in any way he could. Philip told him, however, to ‘stay put’ for the time being. “I will phone you as soon as we have a lead,” he assured him.

After prodding the father some more – who at first was very reluctant to talk about his wife – he let them know the reason why he ended their marriage. “In some ways that whole family – mother, sisters and brothers – are mentally short-changed, if I may call it that. Not all the time, mind you, but in anger they’re not themselves. They had to put her oldest sister into a hospital, as she had become dangerous, killing animals to please God. I found it best for the children to leave. She's two persons in one. Often we lived two lives."

On their flight back, Sonja asked, "What now, Mr. Detective?" She smiled at him with a challenge. "I have to admit, I would be helpless."

"We shall visit that sister in the mental institution," Phil said, then grinned. "Maybe she's not crazy all the time, ha ha."

A day later, they found their patient in the private hospital, and Phil did all the talking. "Tell me, Mildred, who put you in this place?"

"They all did!" she burst out. "They think I'm crazy. Who are you anyway? I never saw you before. Is she crazy, too?" She pointed to Sonja.

"Not yet, my dear, not yet," Phil was trying to appease her, then thought, 'I have to get through her limited conscious shell without causing irritation.'

"Don't dear me, mister; I know you want something from me," she replied.

"We all want something from each other," Phil countered with a laugh, "so why should I hide it?"

Suddenly she laughed out loud, so that one of the nurses rushed into the room. But when Phil and Sonja also began to laugh in the same fashion, she left again, not suspecting anything wrong.

"We sure got rid of her again!" Phil joked. "Are your sisters also that serious when they visit? And their children? They never laugh, hey?"

"Ho, ho, ho, ho, they all think I'm stupid, ha ha." Poking the thumb to her chin, she winked at Phil and whispered, "The poor kids, the little ones." Then, with an even quieter voice, "But I helped one to see God early." She nodded with satisfaction and pride.

Suddenly it began to dawn on the detective and he had an inkling of what might've taken place. He patted Mildred on the arm, winking back at her, then said, "You are not stupid to me. Smart people understand each other. Hey, don't tell them we had this conversation, Mildred," he suggested with a subdued voice; "they wouldn't understand it anyway." Shaking her hand with a grin, the two left.

Inside the car, Sonja asked, "Why did you leave so hurriedly? I could've asked her more questions."

"Think, my dear Sonja, think; you heard her last whisper, too," he said without further explanation. "When we come home, go over your notes again. What did Audry say about their early childhood, when all of them were still in their mother's care at home?"

Sonja tried to prod her mate into revealing what he suddenly had come to perceive during his talk with Mildred, but he said, "No, my beloved one, you're on your own. That's the best way to learn this trade. In the morning we'll go once more to the Lee's place, and with my new understanding, we might discover something."

"Ah, you're back, Mr. Wilbock, still trying to find a clue," Mrs. Lee greeted Phil and Sonja. "Tomorrow you'll have the whole house for a week, we're going to one of my sister's on Vancouver Island. You haven't found my husband, I presume? There're too many Lees in San Francisco to find the right one. For what we know, he might've left from there with our son, Tyler."

Phil didn't answer, and thought, 'We might find your son here, Mrs. Lee, but very dead.' Then he offered, "If we have a whole week by ourselves, Mrs. Lee, we shall not disturb you now. Enjoy the week with your sister on the Island."

Two days later, Philip woke up his mate very early with the word, "I had a short dream a moment or so ago; it wasn't a dream, per se, but a picture moved past my mind, and in it I saw the surface of a dew-covered lawn … it could've been at the Lee's place. At daybreak everything looked even, except one spot, close to a round flowerbed. Get dressed quickly, please, and let's go."

"It's still dark, Phil, we –"

"You want to come or not?" he interrupted her, rather harshly. "That's our work, madam." He walked downstairs to brew coffee and make toast.

"Ah, the smell of that coffee sure wakes me up," Sonja said, as she glanced at him and sat down at the table.

"It's important to be at Mrs. Lee's house the moment the sun gets up, that's how I saw the picture." Phil then ushered Sonja into the garage.

"Yes, I recognize this now, although it's still dark." Phil was satisfied. They positioned themselves behind a window, overlooking the whole lawn area at Mrs. Lee's house, including the round flowerbed.

"Try to look for anything uneven, out of the ordinary, where the dew on the grass shimmers differently from the rest," Phil said quietly to his mate.

As it slowly became light outside, Sonja pointed out the window, "Hey, Phil, you see that patch there? It's on this side of the flowerbed."

"Yes, you're right. Boy, your eyes are good," he called out. Then, "Let's get a shovel out of the basement; hopefully we can find one."

Equipped with a spade, Phil carefully lifted a shovel of grass sod off, to be put back later on, without showing any disturbance on the lawn. One and a half feet down, his spade hit some clothing, then, working with his hands, he uncovered the decaying face of a baby, no doubt the remains of the twin, Tyler.

Wiping his hands on the grass, he said to his partner, "It's still smelling. It probably happened only a month or two ago. That's as far as we do our bit; the rest is for the police."

Sonja was visibly shaken, when she asked, "But how did you suspect this, Phil? I never would've thought of the baby being dead."

"Come, let's go inside," he urged her. "Remember Mrs. Lee telling us that her crazy sister, Mildred, when still very young kids, always tried, and often did, kill their pets by telling them that 'God loves them so much, they had to go early?' Well, being the oldest one, she must've had quite a hold on her little siblings. So, when Mildred in the hospital told us that she had helped one of the little kids 'to see God early', I at once suspected she might've suffocated Tyler on her lap. But Audry Lee, suddenly realizing what had happened, probably was so distraught and in emotional pain at the time, that she left the hospital, pretending the twin boy was asleep. I don't know how she got that make-believe past her oldest daughter, except by saying the father had kidnapped the baby.

"Now then, let's phone Sergeant Whetherby; hopefully, he's at his office already."

Phil also phoned Gordon Lee in San Francisco, telling him what he had found, and Lee's first words were, "I'll take the children; they shouldn't be with their mother right now. So, I'd better come there quickly."

When the detective's police friend entered the house, he said, "Gee, Phil, what's next? We have enough on our hands without you guys." He gave him his old grin.

Sonja injected, "I had nothing to do with this. In fact, I was in the dark, until he dug up the baby's body at sunrise."

The sarge chuckled. "What does he dig up next? You better watch him, Sonja." The meaning of that could be read in his eyes.

* * *

When Sonja came back from her own place, loaded with filled shopping bags of clothing, to be placed in her bedroom cupboards, she said, "For some time now I've had two questions on my mind and today I'm going to put them to you, Phil. Let me first bring these bags upstairs, and hopefully your answers will be positive." With a secret grin she marched past him.

After she had joined him in the living room, she began, "This back and forth between my place and your house is not very accommodating, Phil, so, do you think I could move in with you for good?" Now it was out; what would he say?

Displaying his usual smile, he replied, "I have been contemplating the matter, but thought the suggestion should come from you. I never make any difference between us two; as you know, our rights are equal. Whether man or woman, young or old, I like to see us on the same stage of this life. However, there is a large age factor between us and it cannot be ignored, reason enough for <u>you</u> to approach me, and today you did. Of course, Sonja, I welcome you into this house of mine, and from now on it'll be <u>our</u> house, together."

With tears in her eyes, she seated herself beside him, to rest her head on his chest, listening to his heart.

Then, a few moments after this heartfelt interlude,

she livened up and mused, “So we were brothers in that life, scooting down a long hill ... today we love differently, though, don’t we?”

“Well, perhaps,” he replied, in thought. “There’re different states and stages of love; as souls we express our love much higher up the ladder of consciousness, as I’ve explained previously. I like to believe that our love today comes from soul, where age, as in our case, plays no role; our hearts simply know.”

Sonja followed it up with the words, “But you also said that in marriage the physical love plays a role, too, by expressing that way heart and soul love, to balance the physical relationship. You think there is much difference, if at all, whether we two are married or not?”

“Of course not. Often marriage is only a ceremony, recorded on paper.” Phil patted her harm. “It sure doesn’t make any difference to us, or?”

She simply answered, “I’d like to be married to you, Phil.”

Grinning at her, “That’s the woman in you’ most women would rather get married, and I have nothing against it; in fact, it might even be better, from the viewpoint of the will and some other everyday things society has put upon us, or asks of us. I’m glad the motion came from you, my beloved partner.”

Sonja objected, “But I didn’t suggest it because of the will, or the other things ... as you said, Phil.”

“As if I didn’t know that,” he lamented in jest.

“Now I will table my second question, which is not a question, per se. After all this talk, I don’t know how to put it to you anymore. It’s the woman in me, my feminine desire of wanting to feel you.” She quickly looked up at him. Then, with a deep grin, “I’m not in the dark with this, as I was in our last case, Alexander.”

“I hear your, Alexandra,” he agreed, grinning.

With her head down on his chest again, she whispered, “I want your physical love, too, Phil. With our love of soul, it will balance our relationship, as said. Men only loved me with their sexual desires, but with us it must be a beautiful experience. We can take precautions because of my AIDS.”

He put his fingers through her hair and thought, 'I begin to understand her. Of course, she wants the whole spectrum of love, being still in her prime. Having been short-changed all her life in that regard, now she wants to know and feel how a real physical relationship is. How can I blame her and it certainly will not diminish our love we've experienced so far. Besides, admit it old boy, you want her that way, too. You're a long way from being physically dead.'

The argument Phil had on his lips first, was completely forgotten, and working his fingers firmly through her hair and over her skull, he said, "We shall love as other couples do, and much more. How could we live together under the same roof without it?"

"Oh, Phil, oh, Phil, I love you so much." And her arms slowly moved around his waist, to hang on tightly for a while. Their knowing, and their feeling was synchronized and harmonious.

* * *

Many of Sonja's belongings wound up in the spacious attic of Phil's house. "You live in a much friendlier environment," she said, "more practical, particularly in the kitchen. Perhaps I was old-fashioned in many ways and hung on to some of the stuff longer than necessary. Eventually, I'll get rid of it, and a garage sale will do nicely."

In about a week, the couple had settled into the large house, and when they announced their wedding plans to Sergeant Whetherby, it made the rounds like wildfire. There was absolutely no way to wiggle themselves out of a large party, and the only place suitable to have it was Philip's big house. But there was nothing to worry about, because all of the policemen's wives and friends' wives took care of almost everything, making sure the couple stayed out of their way, by telling them to sit down and relax.

There were at least as many people present as at their previous party, if not more. Since neither Sonja nor Phil were associated with any church, a licensed police officer performed the unforgettable ceremony in their back yard.

Then the party was well on the way when Sonja wanted to address the crowd, and she said with a hoarse voice:

"He made me do this. First I said, 'you do it, Phil,' but he said, 'no, you do it, Sonja.' That went back and forth for a while … Well, here I am with a piece of paper in my hand and shaking. Anyway, the most wonderful thing I got from falling in love with this man is all his friends, all of you, the way you're ready to help, your honesty and your ethics. He wanted me to add ethics," she tried to smile, but instead, tears rolled down her cheeks.

"Looking at this paper again, I also added love," she tried to continue with obvious difficulty. "I can feel your love. You must excuse me … my emotions make me cry, you're all so wonderful."

Phil got up and put an arm around her for comfort. A moment later he said into the quietness, "Hey, cheer up, you guys, we're all right. It seems my partner was right, after all; I should've done it. Do we men ever learn?" Now everybody was laughing.

Speaking up once more, Phil said, "Now you know where our hearts stand, but we also know where your hearts are located." There was a loud applause. He finished with the words, "You're the greatest, and we love you."

How can one describe the vibrations of a wedding party like that? A question very difficult to answer. The hearts of the participants were the cause, creating a love flow nobody could explain.

Early the next morning, the happy couple left the city for their honeymoon, driving east toward Edmonton, where they first had met at the large mall.

Sonja made the suggestion by saying, "I'm not trying to remind myself of the terrible state I was in before I met you. No, my reasons are, that you started me off on a brand new road of hope, of stability, of so much knowledge, and most of all, of love. You gave my life back to me, Phil, and there at the mall it began."

Putting his arms around her, he added, "Yes, my beloved wife, it was not by chance we two met there. The ever-present spirit was the initiator, because we knew from before, and the time had come to be together again in this life." Then, with his old grin, he added, "Let's see how we are going to fashion it."

Chapter 9

The Interrupted Honeymoon

"Did you see that flash of light there in the woods?" Phil asked his wife, as they were driving along.

Twilight was just about upon them and they were driving the last leg toward Calgary, where they intended to stay overnight, before proceeding to Edmonton.

A mile down the highway, Phil stopped the car and said, "I saw this flash in among the high trees on the right and have a hunch that somebody might need some help. You stay here, Sonja, and relax, while I walk back and see; after hours behind the wheel, I can use the exercise."

He came upon a truck and a woman beside it, so he asked, "Can I be of any help, madam?"

However, before she could answer, Philip Wilbock got a blow on his head and lost consciousness.

The woman said, "Why did you have to do that? Stupid you! You might've killed him."

"I know what I'm doing," a man replied, "and don't stupid me, or I'll kick you in the bum."

Tightening up the body on the ground with a long rope around and around, and then taping his mouth, the man said with satisfaction, "He's mine. You look after your girl and give her a sleeping pill, while we drive over the border. I helped you to get her from the old man, now you do your part."

"But that doesn't include killing," she tried to argue.

"He's not dead," was his stoic answer.

"I want to go back to my dad," the girl's voice whimpered.

"Don't worry, darling, I love you, too," the woman tried to calm the little girl they had kidnapped.

At that moment, Phil regained consciousness, to find himself bound like an Egyptian mummy, while his mouth was taped shut.

"He's awake, see that?" the man laughed. "I'd better put him into his 'bedroom', so they won't find him at the border crossing." Picking up the stiff Phil, he shoved him into the hidden compartment under the two-ton truck, closing the lid behind him.

"Come on, let's go," the man urged the woman with the little girl, not older than four years. "I want to cross into the States before daylight in the morning."

Phil was extremely uncomfortable in his narrow compartment, called 'bedroom' by his abductor in a mocking voice. His head was humming like a turbine and his forehead was throbbing as if hammered on continuously with a soft object.

'So they're driving across the border,' he thought, 'and he made sure I can't move nor shout.' Then, 'They probably kidnapped the girl and I got in the way. But why not just leave me there, bound and gagged? Oh, poor Sonja … well, at least they didn't get her. Hopefully, she contacted the police at once and did not walk back to look for me.'

* * *

After her first anxious worry about Phil, Sonja was overcome by a surprising calm, while telling herself, "As I know Phil, he would not leave me here for such a long time without letting me know what he was up to or what happened. No, I'm sure he's in trouble, somebody might've kidnapped him … I really don't know. I'd better flag a car."

As soon as she had left the vehicle, fortunately, a Mounted Police cruiser approached and they saw her waving in the headlights. The driver stopped and backed up to investigate.

With a very calm voice, Sonja tried to tell her story, and before the two officers could ask more questions, she explained, “You see, my husband is a private detective and very inquisitive, but it’s always to help people in need, whether he gets paid or not. So he walked back to where he had seen a flash of light, to be of help, perhaps. But now he’s already gone over an hour, and I didn’t want to go back on my own because of possible danger.”

“You did well, madam, to stay here,” one of the policemen said. “If you come with us, we shall investigate.”

They finally found the tire marks of a heavy truck, but there was no struggle of any kind. “They must’ve taken him by force,” Sonja commented. “For fifty years he’s been a detective and often works with the local police together to solve difficult cases. You can contact Sergeant Whetherby of the Vancouver central office, there he’s well-liked. In fact, they just married us two days ago, and we were on our honeymoon. Some honeymoon.”

Finally, Sonja broke down and cried, as it was simply too much for her emotions to handle. One of the Mounties drove her car to Calgary, while she rode in the cruiser.

There was an all-points bulletin about a possible kidnap, accompanied with a detailed description of Philip Wilbock. However, not the slightest sign of his whereabouts could be found. Sonja was hanging on, though, hoping against all odds that her mate was still well and alive; he simply would not just vanish like that.

She stayed in her hotel in Calgary, every day contacting the police for some message from her beloved husband, to no avail. And often she was thinking about their dream they had had together, which gave her courage. They could not be ripped apart so soon again, she believed that with all her heart and soul.

* * *

Under a terrible strain and some pain, Phil tried to follow the outside events with his ears. He heard when they crossed the border into the United States. Many hours later, he detected through a narrow slit that it had become daylight. As he got used to all the physical discomforts, his nose began to become active. There was a terrible smell in his narrow compartment, that of human excrement, and he added to it by having to urinate.

‘I never was in this kind of a position before, and what

did I do wrong to be in it?' he asked himself. 'What is the lesson I'm learning out of this? I don't believe in accidents, there must be some lesson in this also. What is spirit trying to pass on to me? I simply cannot imagine that this should be the end of my physical life.'

It could've been hours later when Phil's thoughts began to work again: 'All right, spirit, in spite of this awkward position I got myself into, I'm still a strong believer in your validity. Of course, you're still there and so is God. Is there any way to let me know what your intentions are? I'm still willing to do your bidding.'

At that moment a very bright light appeared in Phil's inner vision, and the following was impressed into his soul and mind: 'I am all powerful, all knowing, all present. Coming out of the Godhead, I keep everything alive, by being in everything. I am soul in you, even after your body is gone, which is only one of soul's instruments. I am also Love, soul's most instrumental heritage to grow and mature. Love all and you love me, the Holy Spirit and God.'

For a long while, Phil could hear the sweet sound of a flute, and it gave him the most exhilarated feeling. His agonies and pains were gone. 'I feel as if I'm in heaven,' he thought, 'not that I claim I know heaven.'

After a short, but very bump ride on what must've been a gravel road, the truck finally came to a stop. Phil could hear the loud voice of a woman, "Don't take him out yet, I don't want Rosalyn to see him...." She paused, and more subdued, added, "if he's still alive." Then, "Come on, get my car out of the barn. It takes me at least two days to drive to Magdan."

"Why in such a rush?" he objected, "a day longer or not, what's the difference."

"I know what you want, but I told you already I have my days," she snapped. "Besides, I don't want her to see what you do with him. She's in enough fear."

After the man had backed the car out of the barn, he said, "I wish we had your New Mexico weather up here in Oregon. I don't like the cold."

"You can visit me, but take your time," she suggested, "I want her to settle down first."

All their conversation was welcome information for the ears of the detective.

After she had started the car, Phil was not able to hear their voices anymore.

With the vehicle gone, the man opened Phil's compartment and dragged him out, "How did you like your ride, Mister Detective? I bet you never rode in that kind of comfort," he sneered, while giving the body on the ground a kick.

Cutting the rope off his legs, he said, "I'm not carrying you into your new home: come on, walk, old goat."

Very weak, Phil tumbled into a basement entrance, where the man pointed to a heavy wooden door, "There, in there you'll rot. The rats will keep you company." He slammed the door closed.

Phil's first impression was this awful smell again of human excrement, and he thought, "I bet that criminal had other human beings in here and starved them to death. No doubt, he's one of those senseless killers, getting pleasure out of ... out of what? He might try something else on me, to see me die slowly."

It took the prisoner at least two hours to get all the tight rope off his body and the tape off his mouth. 'What now, Mister Detective?' he asked himself.

The building was an old-fashioned blockhouse, made to last a hundred years. However, time had shrunk parts of the wood, here and there, and he was able to look through those openings, although small. The widest one was half an inch and there, down below this location, he saw part of a town, with several hundred houses perhaps, way out of his calling distance. He was stuck, all right.

Inside the small room, Phil discovered an old vanity and a cot without a mattress; at least he didn't have to sleep on the cold floor. He wetted his lips with water dripping out of a crack to still his thirst.

For two days there were no noises above, so Phil presumed that the man either went into town or lived in another building. When he saw on the third day a shaft of sunlight slowly making its way into his room through the half-inch wide slit, he suddenly was hit by an idea to use it. He could reflect it with the large vanity mirror, to make somebody in town aware of his presence. But the mirror was much too big and clumsy. By the time he finally had broken off a piece, the sun shaft had almost moved out of the slit, out of position.

'Hopefully, the sun will be out again tomorrow,' he thought, then, 'What can I do in the meantime? Oh yes, I will love everybody. I love Mrs. Lee and Dr. Jacoby. I love Doctor Heinreich, in spite of his criminal act. Oh, and I love you, of course, my darling Sonja. And ... and ... yes, I love this man, who wants to starve me to death now, and who makes me so thirsty that I could scream. His soul has a bad enough time putting up with him.' He fell into a stupor-like slumber.

Anxiously awaiting the next day, Phil lingered behind the slit with the piece of mirror in hand. 'During university and taking the courses on criminology, some of us young men taught ourselves the Morse code, and I still remember most of it. I still can do the word HELP,' he was telling himself. 'Somebody in town might see it, or even be able to read it.'

As soon as the sun was in position, he sent out his signal: Di, di, di, di for H; di for E; di, da, di, di for L; and da, di for P. He did that as long as the sun was in position, thinking, 'The people in this little town probably think that that guy up the hill is crazy anyway.'

However, in the late afternoon, a police car drove up the hill, and soon after the voices of the policemen and the house owner – who had appeared out of nowhere – could be heard. This went back and forth, until the lawmen demanded to see inside the house. At that moment, Phil shouted as loud as possible through the slit: "Help! Help! Help! I'm..." But several shots drowned out his voice.

Not too sure what to think, because the scene was out of his sight, he kept quiet. A few moments later, a loud voice asked, "Where are you? I'm the police."

"Down here in the basement," his hoarse voice replied.

With the lock on the door broken open, a groggy Phil walked out and asked the policeman, "Please, can I have some water, I haven't had any for over five days."

While Philip drank greedily, the policeman pointed to the dead body on the ground and explained, "I had to shoot the guy. He shot first and wounded my man. Just relax, if you can, the ambulance is on its way."

"It might interest you," Phil tried to explain, "that I was kidnapped in Canada and brought down here in his big truck."

The policeman shook his head and said, "You were lucky, a ham radio operator saw your Morse Code and phoned us at once. For some time we've tried to catch this fellow in his shady dealings, and I didn't trust him anyway, so had my gun ready, but he hit my partner first. It's not too bad, though, only an arm wound."

At the little hospital, Phil asked the friendly policeman, "I wonder, whether you can contact the Canadian police as quickly as possible, as we were on our honeymoon, and my wife hasn't got a clue as to my whereabouts. The Calgary police or the RCMP would be best."

An hour and a half later, Philip heard Sonja's crying voice on the phone. "Oh, Phil, oh, Phil! I never gave up on you. I simply could not imagine you being dead! You're too smart for that."

"I have to confess something to you, my beloved wife and partner," Phil said slowly into the phone, "I wasn't very smart in dealing with this case. However – and that's the most important thing in our life – soon we'll be together again. And please, please, drive slowly, Sonja. We've had enough with my disappearance."

* * *

When Sonja entered the hospital room, a day later, all that Phil did was open his arms and she sank sobbing onto his chest. So they remained for a long time without words. Their hearts did the feeling, and their souls the communicating.

After their individual stories had been told, Sonja finally said, "Let's forget the whole thing happened; it's too ugly and too violent."

"You're right about the last part," Phil reflected, "but we have to finish the job, my dear partner. I still see the face – if only for a second – of the little girl, calling for her dad; the fear and anxiety it displayed. Now, we adults, and especially I as a detective, have the responsibility to help link her up with her father again. As far as I could make out during this short time, that woman never would be a good mother. The fact already that she hired this criminal to do her bidding, is reason enough for me to go after her; she does not deserve, nor is suited, to raise that girl as her daughter. Hopefully, you're with me, my wife and apprentice."

"And I had made other plans," she said shyly, then grinned at him; "but how could I not see it your way, my beloved Philip, my beloved Alexander?"

"Ho, ho, Alexandra!" He pulled her down on his chest. "That says a lot." His fingers played lovingly with her hair. They could hear their synchronized hearts. Then he said more quietly, "You know I had a close communication with spirit during my time of agony, and at a more appropriate time I'll tell you my experience. It was during my time of pain and physical hardship below the truck. I then sent out my confidence and belief in spirit – this God-like force – in spite of my suffering, and it came through. It was the most wonderful experience I've ever had. I believe now, that my being kidnapped was not in vain, if only to save that little girl. I begin to see the overall picture of why and what we're here for in our physical universe."

Before Sonja left for her hotel room, Phil said, "My nurse does her best to feed me well, but it's only a small hospital. I could use something a bit more nutritious, if you know what I mean; something more nourishing for my old system. You know what we ate at home. I still feel awfully weak, but want to get out of here soon."

"I'll get you something, my husband; don't forget, though, your body hasn't seen food for days, and you don't pick up your old strength overnight."

The next day, the police came a couple of times to get all kinds of information from Phil. Hearing that he was a detective from Vancouver with a lot of experience under his belt, they hoped to obtain some ideas or suggestions from him about this criminal their chief had shot, to get a lead to something they had not thought of yet.

So Philip said, "I have a deep down suspicion about this man, that he might've starved other people to death in his basement prison. There was an awful human excrement stench when I entered that room. I ask you how it got there? If you start digging on his property, it wouldn't surprise me if you find human remains."

Two days later they had dug up five human bodies on the man's farm, with only bones and some clothing left, so he must've been at this business for some time. Suddenly, Phil became an instant celebrity. The small local paper was full of Philip Wilbock and the terrible ordeal he had to go through, interrupting the hardly begun honeymoon with his young wife.

"I feel embarrassed with all the flowers they even send me now," he remarked to Sonja. "What did I do? I let myself be kidnapped, that's nothing to brag about. We'd better get out of here, the sooner the better. One thing I have to say for the local police, though, instead of raking in all the praise, they simply point to me. If it hadn't been for that criminal, I would say that we experienced here the good, old, innocent and honest country life."

A week later, the couple left town one early morning, to make sure it would be quick. However, they left a letter of thanks to the town's people at the hotel desk. In part it said, "We're very grateful for your goodwill and love. You were so kind to us and we thank you with all our hearts. Goodbye."

Having crossed the state border into New Mexico, where they hoped to find the woman and the little girl, they spread out a blanket in the grass, fifty or so yards away from the highway, to enjoy their lunch in the unobstructed sun. Phil was studying a map to find the town the woman had mentioned and was heading for.

Soon they were joined by a tall highway patrol officer, who said, with the most serious face, "I'd better warn you, there's a killer on the loose and he might be carrying a weapon."

Introducing himself and Sonja, Phil gave the officer a brief story of his kidnapping; that they were looking for the woman with her daughter who had been the cause of it. "I thought I heard her say Madanly, or similar, but there is no town in New Mexico with that name or related to it on this map."

Showing much interest in their case, the highway

patrolman said, "I could put it on the air, over our statewide police radio. Somebody might've seen a woman with a distraught little girl. About four years old, you'd say?"

"Yes, I judged her to be that old."

Two days hence, they were stopped by another friendly highway patrolman, who laughed, "I didn't stop you because of any infractions, don't worry, but are you Mr. and Mrs. Wilbock?"

"Yes, yes," Phil answered, wondering how he knew their name.

"Well, sir, we think we might have a lead on the woman and her daughter you were searching for," came the explanation. "The name of that town is probably Magdalena. We're not looking very friendly on people or even parents who kidnap children, so let us know, please, how you make out." He tipped his hat and walked back to his cruiser.

"Yes, darling," Phil couldn't help saying; "we do rather well with our uniformed contemporaries, the way they're willing to help."

The roadmap showed them the way to the town of Magdalena, where they roomed in a comfortable motel, to plan their next steps.

After several days of asking around very inconspicuously, a women was pointed out to them, and Phil recognized her at once, but her daughter was not in sight at that moment. They staked out the house with their car early in the morning, to discover that the woman was bringing the girl to a kindergarten.

"Now we have to get the father from Canada down here," Phil said, planning their next step. "To begin with, we have to find him; who is he? All we know is he lives in Vancouver."

"That might be the most difficult part," Sonja suggested.

"You're right," he agreed. "If we put ourselves into the father's shoes, what would we have done, after the disappearance of his daughter? Pictures!" he called out. "He would've put pictures of her all over the city and beyond. Obviously, you're the one who has to take the girl's picture, to be sent to Vancouver. To be on the safe side, I don't want to be seen at all."

As the children were playing outside, Sonja befriended the kindergarten teacher, who had no objections to let her take some pictures of the happy youngsters, and she took a whole roll of film. It worked out to be simpler than they had anticipated.

Phil recognized at least two good pictures of Rosalyn, and they had them blown up. Then he phoned his friend, Sergeant Whetherby, in Vancouver, and asked how best to go about the situation.

"Look, Phil," a dry voice came over the phone, "we're simply too busy for a thing like that."

"I know, I know, Will," was the quick reply. "I didn't mean you should handle this. How about the policemen's wives?"

"I'll get back to you," he replied and hung up.

The next telephone call came from the sergeant's wife, Wanda. "What gives, Phil? You're not in any trouble? The way Will was talking –"

"No, no, Wanda," Phil chortled, "maybe he was a bit annoyed. But here is the situation." And he told her what his intentions were and how they had come about. Would she and some of the other ladies be willing to help?

"Oh, Phil, many of us wives often wondered how we could help to bring those kidnapped kids back to their parents. Now you give us the opportunity. Send us a fax with the girl's picture and name, we'll do the rest."

Three days later, Wanda called back, "We're in luck, Phil and Sonja, I have Fred Hauser right beside me and he recognized his daughter, Rosalyn. Isn't that marvelous? Here, I'll let you speak with him."

"It's a wonder that you found my daughter down there, so far south, Mr. Wilbock. You know, the Canadian and American courts gave me the children, all four of them, because of their mother's incoherence and incompetence, to the point of being violent. I thought I'd never see my youngest one again, and I thank you from the bottom of my heart. I'd best fly down to Albuquerque; that's probably the closest airport, and drive from there to Magdalena."

It was a very happy reunion of daughter and father,

who, with a court order in hand and the local police at his side, picked up his four-year-old one late afternoon, at the doorstep of his former wife's house.

When the women saw Philip, she probably wished she could sink into the floor, but the police already had charged her with kidnapping, and Phil didn't want to add to that. His honeymoon, although violently interrupted for over two weeks, was rather on his mind. "To somehow get even with that woman," he said to his wife, "is not in my stars; I'd rather be free."

Later on Phil asked Sonja, "Oh, my beloved one, have you an idea of how this case makes me feel? I have accomplished something in the spiritual sense, too. I simply could not disregard the deep and awkward pain of the little girl – if only seen in a flash – and now my heart and soul are jubilant over the happy ending."

They decided to have their honeymoon in the warmth of the south. When driving past a large hospital in Tucson some days later, Sonja suddenly called out, "I want to have my AIDS tested, whether it's still there and positive."

Phil grinned at her, "The intuition of a woman. We might be in for a surprise." Inside the building, he suggested, "Get a double-check; they make mistakes, you know."

To their complete amazement, there was not even a trace of AIDS left, and doctors wondered that she could've had it in the first place.

Before they drove the car out of the underground parking lot, Sonja pulled Phil close to her and said, "And now, my husband and lover, I want a kiss, a long kiss, from lips to lips.

All possible happiness was manifested and came to bear in this so-often-missed union of their lips.

Chapter 10

The Next Classroom In Our World

The happy couple hardly had arrived at their home on Adler Street and were in the middle of unpacking the suitcases and bags when the phone rang; it was Sergeant Whetherby. "Boy, oh boy, what took you so long to get home? we–"

"Look, Will," Phil interrupted him, "you were the ones who sent us on a honeymoon, and, after a very violent interlude, we took it easy. I seem to remember that a certain sergeant was kind of short up when I phoned him from New Mexico and –"

"Yes, yes, yes," the sergeant stopped the detective quickly; "I know, I know … I was very busy then and already had a verbal licking from my wife because of that, Phil. But now –"

"It's all forgotten, old boy," Phil said, laughing; "I'm not trying to rub it in. But kidnapped children have a right, too, and I'm glad Wanda and the other ladies have formed an organization now to look after that."

"I'm glad about that, too, my friend," the sergeant replied. "Did you guys have a good time? Some day you've got to tell me all about the kidnapping. And now –"

"Slow down, Will, slow down; yes, we had a wonderful time. Your voice is telling me, though, that we're back again and right down into business."

Will laughed, "Right you are, back to the present, Phil, and your help is urgently wanted. We need the dog, but Mrs. Eisen will not loan it to us without you. She says, and I quote: 'The only person who has any right to my Tom, beside me, is Philip Wilbock. Maybe Sonja, too, his helper.' So, there you have it. She has a mighty respect for you and I can see her point. Hopefully, in the near future, we'll have our own little dog with Tom's abilities. The drug haul a few months ago, really has started the stone rolling in that direction."

A moment later, he continued, "The main reason I'm calling, Phil and Sonja, is that we could use Mrs. Eisen's dog now. It's kind of complicated to tell you everything on the phone, but if you could come in tomorrow morning around eight to headquarters, we will go from there on."

"Good, Will, good. We're unpacking right now and want to settle down first. See you then."

The next morning Sergeant Whetherby received the two with a smile, a handshake and, "Welcome home."

Then he invited them to a ride in his police car, as he explained. "They leave us alone in there and nobody can listen in. The Jewish community in town is upset because somebody took it upon themselves – we strongly believe there're several people involved – to smear, deface and even destroy their property. It started off with the synagogue. then some of their homes and now the Jewish cemetery. It appears this anti-semitism is spreading to some of the high schools, most likely only a fad with the kids there. If we could've caught the people who started it in the beginning, it might not have taken off as it did. But, unfortunately, we missed the boat, being so busy with more serious crimes."

A moment later, he continued, "Now the higher ups are on our backs, as you can imagine. I personally think that Mrs. Eisen's dog probably would've led us to those criminals, but she wouldn't give it to us, and now it's too late. By now she probably wishes she had loaned us her dog, being a Jew herself, but there is no turning the time back. I took you on this ride, away from the office, because there hasn't been a quiet moment anymore. Every time one of the bosses – some have taken it upon themselves to act like it – comes in sight, they want to discuss this subject and give advice, plenty of it, as if they have all the experience in the world. It's disgusting, Phil, Sonja."

Then, "Their egos are flying high, and if they would see you getting involved in this 'show-biz of the intellect' – that's what it has become – I never would hear the end of it. During our drive here we're safe. You know, I've thought of early retirement, but I'm not a person who's ducking his responsibilities, in spite of all the flak they're dishing out right now. So, there it is. Perhaps you, Phil, can come up with something I haven't thought of, but you have to be on your own, or let me know in secret, for reasons I just mentioned. Some of those fakes never would forgive me, if they found out I work with you two; because they seem to have a lot of pull, I keep my mouth shut."

"Ha, ha, Will," Phil laughed, "we know all about that. We've done it before and will do it again this time, as if we hardly knew each other. You sure have my … our support, and we'll go to work as soon as possible. I've got a case right now and have to take it first, but then we're free to work underground, ha ha, so don't worry, my friend." They parted at headquarters.

* * *

A distraught mother was worried about her fifteen-year-old daughter, who had run away, and her husband, the girl's stepfather, was very adamant about his choice. "If that daughter of yours wants to be on her own, or rather with her boy lover, I won't lift a finger to get her back." But the mother was not at all sure that it simply was a case of running away; she knew her daughter better; deep down in her heart she was convinced that there might be a reason for the girl's sudden departure without letting her know.

"I think we need Tom for this case," Phil said to Sonja, "so, let's go to Mrs. Eisen first and pick him up."

Naturally, Welda Eisen was full of all the events concerning the Jewish community, being a Jew herself, and she commented very emotionally: "What can we do? Those crazy people who started it, now seem to find support from the young in our town, and to them it's nothing but a present-day rage, of course, to be funny and do something lunatic. I don't know, Phil, were we that way, too? It's the violent time of today. I wonder if I should've let the police have the dog? Tom sure might've done some good in the beginning, shortly after it started."

It seemed Welda didn't want to stop talking and to keep them there for awhile to discuss her issue of deep concern. However, Phil and Sonja were only there to pick up the dog, and if not in a rush, they wanted to get their new case 'rolling'. So Philip said very diplomatically, "You know, Welda, good Tom might still play a big role in solving this whole terrible happening, and we're here to pick him up at once. I see he's wagging his tail already, knowing very well what we're up to."

"So, you're involved in this, too?" she asked, surprised.

"You'd better believe it, my friend," Phil put his arm around her shoulder. "But it has to stay a secret. We had a long talk with Sergeant Whetherby, and now know the implications. Some politicians seem to be on the back of the police, so it's best to stay in the background. We just came back from our honeymoon yesterday, and you can imagine our surprise when we heard this."

Walking toward the house door, Phil said, "You must forgive us, Welda, that we can't stay longer, but time is essential, and so far it has not been on the side of the law."

Welda Eisen put her arms around the couple. "I know you will find the perpetrators and good Tom probably will do his part again. Bye-bye, my beloved doggy...." She patted him and sent them off with a concerned smile.

At the time nobody did know that, indeed, Tom would play an important role and do his job. However, first the detective and his assistant had to find the lost girl.

Even more upset than on the phone, Mrs. Lisak received the couple at the house door. "You'd better not come here again, or my husband won't like it at all. Here, I'll give you some money and see whether you can find the girl."

"I don't want your money, not before I have some results," Phil said, refusing to take it. "However, we have to have some information, and how will we be able to communicate with you?"

"Do it by phone," was her immediate answer. "Ring twice, put the receiver down, and ring three more times, then I know it's for me."

As an afterthought, she suggested, "Go to her high school three blocks from here; she has some friends there and they might tell you more."

"She's scared stiff of her husband," Phil said later to Sonja. "I never will know how these people find each other and then stay together."

"People are very lonely, Phil. It's an awful thing to be lonely … I know something about that. They don't mind paying for the negative considerations, if somebody will hold them in their arms, once in a while."

Looking sideways at his mate during the drive, Phil thought, 'She probably went through that a lot before we met.'

At the high school they found a very pleasing principal, who was only too willing to help, and he said with a sad voice, "We knew about Marina; she was not happy with her new father. You can speak with her classmates during intermission in ten minutes, but please, be careful what you say, as some of them are easily offended and then they close up."

Phil was an excellent communicator with juveniles, though, and they opened up when he asked for their help; they readily agreed. It appeared that Marina's father had beaten her at times and even tried to abuse her sexually.

While some of the girls played with Tom, the detective explained, "We have a dog here with a wonderful nose and I wonder whether there is some clothing in this school he can take a sniff of?"

"We will find something in her locker," one of the girls suggested, "but we need the principal with the key to open it."

There was only a blouse and skirt in the locker for Tom to put his nose into, and one of the girls commented, "That's all she ever wore; they never let her have anything better." Meaning her father, of course.

Then Phil asked, "Is there a place, a park with a

wooded area, or empty land without a house, where you went after school, to be among yourselves? You know what I mean?"

"There is the creek bed not too far from here," one of the boys replied; "we go there, but I've seen the girls there, too."

Having opened the locker and still present, the principal said at once, "Why don't you all show Mr. Wilbock where it is, and I'll talk with your teacher."

The whole class then followed on, some of them laughing to have skipped class with the help of their principal. There were dense bushes all along the shallow waterway, and it didn't take Tom very long to lead them to an area on the other side of the water, and it was right to the body of the girl, Marina! It was their classmate all right, but very dead!

Some of the girls began to cry, while Phil had a quick look; perhaps he could find the cause of her death, but nothing was visible, not even on the surfaces of her bare neck.

"We'd better get the police," Philip finally said, his words sounding like a strange language in the quietness. "Would you stay here, Sonja, please?" She just nodded, deeply affected by this appalling event.

"Can I stay here, too?" one of the boys asked; "she was my best friend," and tears rolled down his cheeks.

With the police at the scene, Phil said to one of them, "I have a suspicion and would like to follow it up." At that moment, Sergeant Whetherby arrived and he just shook his head. Then, looking at his friend, he said, with sadness in his voice, "Every week we have this now."

Away from the nosy crowd, Phil said quietly. "We might find the killer soon, Will, as the dog had a good sniff of the girl's clothing, and I strongly suspect her stepfather. Hopefully he's at home."

Then, "With Tom's nose full of the girl's scent, he will bark out a recognition, as he always does. I think I can blunder that man into a confession, if you'll stay out of sight for a moment. I'm also wired, to record what he has to say."

"Good, very good," the sarge said as he led the way to the car; "let's give it a try."

Fortunately, Mr. Lisak was at home for lunch, as they had found out quickly by phone. Upset he came to the house door to see who'd interrupted his meal.

Excitedly, Tom began to bark and the detective followed it quickly, without giving the man a chance to say anything, he harshly shouted: "So you had to get rid of your stepdaughter and kill her! Besides the dog here, we have other proof."

The man became so angry that he went for Phil, shouting out: "You had to find out, you son of the devil. I'm going to kill you the very same way I did that girl!"

That's all they needed! Phil had ducked down promptly to avoid the blow, while the sergeant, with the help of his fellow policemen came in and put shackles on the surprised killer.

Staying out of the main investigations, Phil and Sonja went to the school and had a talk with the principal, who said, "Some of the kids really took it hard and are helpless to cope emotionally. There're other parents, you know ..." he didn't finish his sentence, but the two had an idea what he meant.

"I kind of wondered," Phil began, "what else we could do? I had the feeling that most of the kids wished they could help somehow, to avoid this kind of a crime. Having had this terrible and personal experience, they might look for a lead, some solid advice. I have an idea what that might be and would like to talk to them, as a friend rather, who has seen a lot of this violence; it might give their emotions, hearts and minds relief that they actually <u>can</u> help and <u>do</u> something."

"Would you do that?" the teacher asked with a pleasant surprise in his tone. "I like that, I like that very much. How about tomorrow morning at nine?"

* * *

At home, Phil said to his wife, "I shall phone at least one of the Big Brother mothers; with your AIDS gone, she, and particularly her son, probably will look forward, if I make my appearance again." While dialing the phone, he smiled. "I know I'm welcome there."

When a woman answered, he simply said, "Hi!"

The next thing he heard was, "Is that you, Phil?"

"Yeah, that's him," he said with a grin.

"Oh, I'm so glad you called," the mother answered excitedly, "So often I wanted to call you, but wasn't sure whether I should've. It simply wasn't right that they cut us off because your lady has AIDS; it was not right. With Robert in school now, you don't know how many times he has asked for you. He could not understand the whole thing, and what do I tell him? He's still too young."

"Don't worry, I'll be his Big Brother again," Phil said, calming her. "By the way, the lady in question is my wife now and the AIDS is gone, so there's nothing to be feared anymore."

"What was there to be feared? Fiddle, faddle, they blew everything out of proportion," she huffed.

"This time I'm not going through the Big Brother organization again," he explained, "for reasons I don't want to go into here. You want me back, Thea?"

She laughed, "What kind of question is that? Of course, we want you back, Phil. You just wait, when I tell Robert … you were like a father to him."

"Saturday morning then, at eight," he suggested, "See you at your place."

Well, it was a very emotional reunion and that included the mother, who couldn't resist asking, "Mind if I put my arms around you, Phil? You sure have been missed here."

With the boy on his arm, he asked, "But why didn't you phone? I'm not miles away." Then, to Robert, he asked, "And how do you like school, Robert?"

"I like it," he answered, "and I have three friends already, two boys and one girl. Where are we going today, Uncle Phil?"

"How about Stanley Park?" he suggested. "With snow or rain in the air, we can visit the aquarium, where there's so much to be seen."

Thea called out, "I would like to come along, then we can chat a bit and find out what we've missed."

A moment later, she said with some pride, "By the way, I've a good job now and it's steady, so our finances have improved."

There was so much happiness between the three, and

it seemed to reflect on all people coming near and in contact with them. Robert, however, was happiest; he truly had missed his Big Brother.

When lunch time approached, Phil said, “Because of this special occasion, we'll have our nourishment, if I may call it that, in a good restaurant, and you can order to your stomach's content … it's on me.”

On his way back home, Phil thought, ‘With all the violence I've been in contact with lately, this mother-son team sure gave me a lift, and my inner self needed it. I should've taken Sonja along, too.’

* * *

Phil never could've imagined that his discourses in high school on criminology, protection against crime, detecting criminal acts and criminals, and every subject related to these topics, were so well-liked. In a considerably short time he was asked by other schools whether he could do the very same there for the students, as they seemed to be hungry for it.

Sergeant Whetherby phoned his friend one day, proclaiming, “Boy, we've tried this for years, but our relationship with the youngsters in school is not very good, and I cannot imagine why, Phil? Where did we go wrong?”

“It's that old imprinted illusion, Will,” was the answer; “it started some time ago, probably through a very negative incident. Today it's only an illusion, my friend, but that imprint can be broken. Why not have two or three of your men trained to get a ‘foot into the door’; the opportunity is there now, and I'll do my best to help make the changeover. It's kind of getting over my head, as I'm too busy with other things. Sonja is taking a course now on speech making, to have more confidence in front of a crowd, and be of help to me. She is a wonderful speaker in front of me, but more than ten people give her the creeps. However, we can't do this forever … it's beyond our job.”

“You sure gave me an idea there,” the sarge agreed at once, “and I shall go to work on the matter forthwith. Thanks a lot, old boy.”

“Then I can make the introduction, Will, as soon as

you're ready," was the immediate answer. "Most of the kids trust me completely; I've become their good example, and I can transfer this to your men."

"Yes, yes, excellent," was the satisfied answer.

One day, two boys came to Phil and asked to speak with him in confidence, making sure nobody was nearby. One of them said, "For quite some time we have known who's behind all that violence against the Jews, but were afraid to speak up. We know why you weren't invited to that one high school, because the boys there and some girls also are helping those guys. And if caught squealing, they might come after us."

Then, very quietly while looking around, the other boy whispered, "With what you've told us, we trust you … most of us do, and we know you never would squeal on us. It's the Ku Klux Klan from the States; they have a headquarters here in the city, too, and come to us high school kids to help them. We can give you their address, but you never must mention us. There're others in the schools, but they're afraid to speak out."

"You have my word, young men, your names will never come over my lips," the detective assured them.

'What a lucky break,' Philip thought to himself. 'I will have to do it right and not jeopardize the lives of these kids. Yes, those people are dangerous … employing high school kids for their dirty work; what a bunch of fanatics.'

During this period of high school lecturing and giving discourses, the dog had been with Phil and Sonja almost continuously, to demonstrate the animal's ability to sniff out undetectable things, like very small amounts of drugs or even a cigarette of marijuana. But this school work also had hindered and inhibited his job as a private detective.

When Sergeant Whetherby sent three of his men, in a very short time, to take over his work, he was extremely happy, as the job simply had gone over his head. He had no trouble introducing them, and, because they wore civilian clothing, it did not cause undue attention with the kids. It worked out unexpectedly well.

Now he was a full-fledged private detective once more and could put his vigilance on the Ku Klux Klan, a priority in his mind and heart. But, first of all, he brought Tom back to his mistress, while Sonja was still busy in one of the schools, as the dog needed to be in his home environment for a while and have a rest.

"You're a busy bee, Phil," Welda Eisen greeted him with a deep smile. "I heard about your school work; well done, my friend … the kids need it. Hopefully, you have a few moments for tea?"

"Oh yes, Welda, I have the time," Phil said, as he squeezed past her in the parlor.

Sipping their hot brew and munching the homemade biscuits with pleasure, they spoke of the latest news, nothing too extreme or too violent. It was their time to relax the mind, heart and soul. And Tom, having reclaimed his comfortable box, did not fare less, meeting old friends in his dream world again.

* * *

Of course, the detective had filled in his police friend on what the two boys had revealed to him, but he never could've had secrets of that nature before Sergeant Whetherby.

Almost every week some anti-semitism came to the surface, mainly by spraying paint on houses, public buildings or even on the surface of streets, where everybody could see it. They all were rush jobs, easy for the perpetrators to leave quickly by car.

Then, in late spring, letters arrived in many a Jewish house saying that, from then on fire would be used to wipe out all the Semitic race.

Hearing that, Phil said to Sonja, "That's fanaticism, if I ever heard of it, and they might be dead serious; we'd better get our doggy friend, Tom, back to us. From now on we'll wear our weapons all the time. Their dirty work might also give us the opportunity to nail them for good and lay our hands on some of the high school kids who became the pawns of the Ku Klux Klan. We have some of their home addresses, but never were able to prove their involvement. This might be our time and we'll be ready."

"I kind of wonder whether they've got me marked as a Jew," Sonja questioned. "It kind of makes me shiver to the bone, although we never received letters of threat. I'm not leaving this house during darkness; they're not getting me, my husband, you can depend on that."

"A word of caution, darling," Phil said, trying to calm her emotions, "first of all, we're detectives with good ethics, even against people who claim we're their enemies. We have to keep our shirts on, or we'll fall into the very same category they're in. We're judging by what we see and experience, and not by what our emotions tell us."

"Oh, you're so calm and composed, and I'm glad I have you; I'll try my best," was her answer.

Two days later, somebody tried to torch the synagogue, however, because of the prearranged calling system, the two Wilbocks were there even before the police arrived.

Quickly Tom was led around the building to get his nose full of the 'goodies' necessary to catch the suspects. When Sergeant Whetherby drove up, Phil suggested to his friend, "Tom has his nostrils full already, Will, so all we need now is a squad car to drive to the house of the Ku Klux Klan, and we'll have them nailed. I never was so sure before."

"I'll come myself," was the immediate answer. At the Klan's large house, however, they were confronted with a different development. All the doors were locked tight, and suddenly rifles appeared from behind the shattered glass windows, with the loud voice of a man, telling them: "You'll have to take us by force and die in the process!"

"This is going to be a very serious thing!" the sergeant exclaimed, while backing up the vehicle. "I'd better get more cars."

At that moment, other Klan members arrived at the scene. But before they could run for the house, the sergeant and his men had them covered with their guns. It was only good that at that tense time, four more police vehicles came up to assist, because two more Klan cars had appeared and the officers were very busy apprehending and shackling them.

Fortunately, their leader was one of the prisoners, and he shouted to his men, barricaded in the house: "No use to get yourselves killed. We have other means to get them darn Jews. The fire tonight was only the beginning of our campaign."

Phil and Sonja were busy until the early morning hours, using Tom to trace high school boys to their homes. They were often very sad cases because the parents did not know of their children's negative activities and certainly not in connection with the Ku Klux Klan organization. Many would face expulsion from school later on.

If not put in prison, all Klan members certainly would be extradited back to the States.

A few days later, Sonja experienced an aftermath, while doing some shopping. One of the expelled boys recognized her and began to give her a hard time with foul language. But before he could give her a physical working-over, a mall guard, who had been called to the scene, quickly handcuffed him, so he used his dirty words on him, too.

After having heard her story, Philip said, "Hopefully, in cases like that or similar, with a lot of people around, you never will pull your pistol and even shoot at the attacker. It never works the way you see it on TV. Personally, I rather would take a beating." He winced, then continued, "It'll take some time to straighten out those youngsters again. I'm glad I'm not one of their parents. Regrettably, some of them are so easily led today toward the negative side of their existence. Fortunately, though, most of the kids are turning their heads away from the negative beckoning of our society's pitfalls and violence."

Showing his old smile again, he said, "I'm sure glad I could contribute to the school kids' positive aspects of life. The way it took off, now even the public schools ask for the policemen's discourses. What a wonderful way to give our children a solid foundation, for the time when they have to face adulthood, and the next classroom in our world. From all the situations confronting our lives today, hopefully, they will dig out the positive aspects to guide them, like love, wisdom, humor and compassion, for example."

"Oh, you said that so well," Sonja praised as she cuddled up beside him on the sofa. "And much of it because of a certain smart detective.

Chapter 11

There Is a Higher Law and Court

The Wilbocks enjoyed an early morning hot-tub sitting and a chat, when the telephone rang and a woman's voice said, "2999 Adler, I see you're still there, Phil. This is Mildred McDonald, remember me?"

"Oh, it's you, Mildred," Phil answered, "how can I forget you, even in ten years from now, if I'm still around. What can I do for you this time? Don't tell me you want me to locate your husband again?"

"Ach, you're still on that," she replied, not wanting to be reminded, it seemed. "Which husband did you mean anyway, the fifth or sixth one? No, now it's a woman. We stayed together over two years, and then she was suddenly gone, and I don't know why. I'm not poison. But the thing is, this time, some of my most valuable jewelry is missing."

"So, that mighty love is still escaping you, Mildred," Phil mused; "if I only could help you in that respect, but that's not in a detective's bracket, not mine anyway."

"Look, Phil, you should've married me when I made you the offer," she lamented, "we would've made a perfect pair. My money and your brain, what a match! But you refused, having only the mighty love of yours in mind. And now we're both still single and lonely, too. It's not right; it's not right."

"You've a point there, Mildred, loneliness in one's life is an awful thing," he agreed. "However, my dear lady, I've got a surprise for you … I'm married to the most wonderful girl, and it's love, real love. Right now she's sitting beside me in the hot-tub, soaking our muscles and bones. Hey, why don't you join us? Or are you not in shape yet?"

"What kind of talk is that? I'm always in shape, night or day. I thought you'd know that."

Phil laughed. "Of course I know … I'm just kidding. Are you coming?"

"Yes, yes, yes, that's the best offer I've had in a month!" She laughed, "I'd sure like to meet your wife and get jealous."

When Mildred saw Sonja, she burst out, "Wow! Is that what real love is all about? Gee, I sure missed out on that." And the tall, slender blond, in her sixties already, sank with pleasure into the hot water. "But I can see you're both happy; I have an eye for that."

Settled in, she began, "You think this real love can be between two women? I thought I had found love with Mary. And now this…" She shrugged her shoulders with disgust. "But I only want my jewels back. If you catch her, forget about the police, just the jewels."

In the kitchen, an hour or so later, and then having breakfast, Phil suggested, "I have a feeling that your Mary might leave town by air, so we shall have a stakeout at the airport with our doggy friend, starting this morning. First, though, Tom has to have his nose into some of her clothing at your place. You've got to give us pictures, too."

"You can have all that," she replied. "Her cupboards are full of clothing and I've plenty of snapshots flying around."

It took the detective and his assistant hardly two days to discover Mildred's friend, Mary – that is Tom did – while she was standing in line to buy an airplane ticket to Montreal. Well, after Phil had given Mildred a quick ring, she was there so fast, that one could've thought she had flown to the airport terminal to recover a billion dollars. Sonja and Phil stayed out of their conversation and only waved to Mildred, as the two left the building together.

* * *

There was a call from Sergeant Whetherby, and he explained, "We've been approached by the Middle East community here in town; apparently some of their people have left their homeland by air, but never get here, or get here and then disappear. Gee, Phil, Sonja, I haven't got the manpower to dig into that; besides the RCMP already has interest in the case. The reason I'm calling you is, they asked me, whether I know a good detective. So, I thought about you, of course, but wanted your permission first, if you're interested, then I can give them your name."

Phil replied, "We're free at the moment, Will, there's nothing serious on our itinerary."

"Okay, I'll give them your name and number then," the sarge responded. "Hey, and don't go to the Middle East, you guys, it's too hot there." And he hung up.

They hardly had time to think about it, when the phone rang again. It was an Iranian, Dr. Amman, and, since Sonja had answered the call, he asked, "Could I speak with Detective Wilbock, please?"

Phil replied, "My wife and I work together, Dr. Amman, and since you're on the speaker, we both can hear and speak with you."

"Oh ... all right then," the doctor said with some reluctance. "Sergeant Whetherby probably has explained it to you. Will you take our case? We pay well. However, before you'll agree, I must tell you that some of our members are not very fond of being approached by a woman ... Our old religious customs don't die easily, not even in this western world of equality. If your wife could work in the background ... You know what I mean?"

While Phil grinned toward Sonja, he answered, "Don't worry, Dr. Amman, we understand and will be discreet."

"Good," came the satisfying answer. "Now then, I would like to brief you on all the important points. Could you come to my place, please?"

"Yes, of course," Phil agreed. "Do I have to leave my wife at home?"

"You can bring her," came the answer, "some of us are liberated, as you might call it."

The Wilbocks entered a large and plush home, located in one of the better parts of the city, and were greeted by a servant at the door, who led them into a study. Dr. Amman entered immediately with the words, “In here we're private, some of my smaller children are very inquisitive and always want to meet strangers.”

“Were you born in this country?” Phil asked, “Your English is as good as if you lived here all your life.”

The doctor answered with visible pride, “I was born here in Vancouver; my parents left Iran as a young couple to settle here on the west coast of British Columbia. They both were physicians and brought up eight children, and I'm the youngest. We're all well-educated and some of us have even adopted the Christian faith. One might call it ‘the pull of the western world’. However, to come to the reason of my wanting to hire your services, several of our newcomers have their struggles, particularly when it comes to dividing religion from their daily living. Many other new Canadians have these difficulties too, of course, but we now believe that religious fanatics, with roots in one or all of the Middle East countries, have infiltrated our communities here in Vancouver, and they also operate across the border, as we hear from our friends in Seattle.”

At that moment a male servant entered with coffee and tea, to be served and poured by the host himself. While they were sipping the hot brew and nipping the offered sweets, the doctor continued the dialogue. “This whole affair has become very serious now, in fact, too serious, to be ignored any longer. You see, some of the particularly young people are actually disappearing; they take off from one of the Middle East countries by air, but never get here. It's not on a grand scale, but it happens. We suspect a certain religious group behind it, because they condemn their countrymen for leaving, when their country needs them most. Here in town they approach young people, too, to go back, with very little success, though; once here in North America, nobody wants to go back.”

After some thought, the doctor began once more, “This group's leader probably operates from the Middle East, but has followers and helpers here in town and in the States, who take his orders. For instance, he informs them when a young person, or even a young family is leaving their home country, to take up their new residence here in Canada, particularly here on the west coast. We've tried about all we can to find out how they operate, but..." he lifted his hands, indicating helplessness; "young people are disappearing. Will you help us to solve this mystery, Mr. Wilbock? We don't know where else to turn. Sergeant Whetherby recommended you highly and, hopefully, your ability as an experienced detective can shed some light on this matter of great concern to us."

Inside the car, on their way home, Sonja said, "I really would be stuck with this one, Phil. What now? We can't stake out the airport all the time, and who do we look for?"

"You're long enough with me to know that some of our work, some of our answers, do not come from this knucklehead of ours," he chided her, while putting his index finger to his head. "Often we use our intuition, the voice from within," he poked a finger to her heart.

At home again, he got Sergeant Whetherby on the line. "Hey, Will, this doctor's job will probably keep us busy at the airport for some time. Who do we contact there? You happen to know the policeman in charge?"

Will replied, "We're old friends, it's Detective Caspar Jordine. They're keeping their appearance low-key and all wear civilian clothing. I'll give him a ring and tell him that a certain detective and his wife are prowling around his field of action."

Phil laughed, then said, "We just were there with our doggy friend, Will, but it was a quick job. As usual, good Tom had sniffed out the subject in a hurry. This will be much more difficult, it'll be mind, intuition or bust, in where Tom can't have any part." He signed off with a chuckle.

Two days later, Dr. Amman called the Wilbocks and he said, "We're in luck; our contact in Tehran phoned us that a young family of four has left by air for Vancouver. Although we think that two adults and two little children should be safe enough and not be kidnapped, but just in case ... They should arrive here within three days, because they're visiting some relatives in Germany first. That's all I can give you. Good luck."

Phil commented to his mate, "Well, it's something. Let's establish the arrival times from Germany. That should narrow down our presence at the airport considerably."

Two days later, while waiting at the air terminal for the fourth time already, where the passengers from Lufthansa were to be expected, Phil whispered to Sonja, "See those three Middle East men there? They look awfully suspicious to me."

"But how would they kidnap a family of four?" Sonja whispered back. "They would cause a lot of commotion, wouldn't they?"

Phil replied, "They're not that stupid. There's drugs today available which inhibit the human speech and the physical resistance, they make you docile. After they have injected the two adults with a special, sensitive needle, and before they realize what's going on, they simply lead them off. The children are probably too young to catch on."

"It scares me, Phil," Sonja couldn't help commenting, taking her husband's arm to feel more secure.

When the people began to stream through the gates, Phil said, "Let's simply watch the three guys and see what they do."

He hardly had the words out, and the three Middle East men pushed their way to a young couple with two children on their hands. They did their drug injection job so inconspicuously, that, unless one had his eyes directly on the scene, one would think they had greeted old friends or relatives.

Suddenly Phil had a hunch and he hoarsely said to his mate, "I bet they have a car waiting outside the building, with the doors wide open. I'll rush out, you stay here and follow them." And he walked ahead, pushing and shoving through the crowd.

As he'd suspected, there was a van waiting with the side doors open. The nervous driver looked anxiously toward the doors of the building, and only Phil knew why. He thought, "That man is the fourth of the kidnapping team. His Middle East appearance gives him away."

He sneaked to the back of the van with a little device in hand – part of his everyday detective equipment – and unscrewed the valves of one front and back tire, to let the air escape. The driver had been so busy with his eyes and ears in the direction of the terminal doors, that he had missed out on this happening.

That done, he pulled his cellular phone out of his pocket to call the airport detective. The policeman hardly had arrived to greet Phil, when the loaded van wanted to pull away in a hurry, but it didn't get far. Phil said to the detective, "Watch this," and he pointed to the vehicle, which had veered to the left and came to a sudden stop. "In there you'll find a drugged family and four Middle East men, who are their kidnappers."

Sonja had joined them, while the detective gave orders to his men to apprehend the criminals. Turning around and scratching his head with delight, he asked Phil, "Did you let the air out of his tires? Don't tell me…" he grinned.

Phil nodded with pretended seriousness. The policeman began to laugh out loud. Then he said, "What a way to nail the perpetrators in their act." While his men were busy around the van and an ambulance with a doctor taking care of the drugged couple, he said once more, "You must be Sergeant Whetherby's friend, Detective Wilbock? I'm sure glad to make your acquaintance. The sarge 'warned' me about you…" and he trailed off, laughing again.

Fifteen or so minutes later, the airport policeman approached the Wilbocks again, and he said, "Hopefully this ends that kidnapping drama, which might've gone on for some time."

To the police detective's surprise, Phil replied, "I doubt it! I've noticed other men conversing with them and by their looks they also might've been from the Middle East. My hunch is they belong together. We might get another hint from the doctor who hired us."

"Boy, let me know, please," the policeman expressed his eagerness, "we better get rid of these fanatics."

Later that afternoon, when Sergeant Whetherby called the two, he said, "You know who you caught in that airport haul? A kidnapping ring, as my police friend tells me. Apparently, their religion is opposed to any kind of immigration of their own to the western world. We presume they kill their victims here and then get rid of their bodies. How? We probably never will know because they don't talk."

Phil called Dr. Amman and explained, but warned that, as far as he was concerned, some of the kidnapping ring people were still at large. The doctor was extremely grateful and immediately wanted to find out who that kidnapped family had been, so he could be of help to them. Then he asked, "What else can we do?"

Phil replied, "I honestly don't know. The airport police is on guard now and know what to look for. It's a ticklish situation, though, with all your country folks running around the terminal every day; how does one identify the real perpetrators, not knowing who to expect from any of the Middle East countries?"

"I understand, of course," the doctor answered, "but I would like to keep you on the case, if you don't mind, because I have the feeling you might catch the others."

"All right, Dr. Amman," Phil agreed; "but do understand, please, we cannot stake out the airport every day for twenty-four hours."

A week or so later, and having visited the airport terminal almost every day, the Wilbocks were at it again, when two men of Middle Eastern descent caught their eyes, and Phil said, "I don't like their looks. Let's follow them."

When the passengers from a British arrival poured through the gates, the two men suddenly moved toward a girl, and took her between them. "This is too obvious to ignore," Phil said to Sonja. "Look at the girl ... she didn't know what hit her. The drug works awfully fast. Now they move her along by her elbows; see that?"

As they put themselves on their tail, Phil said, "I better call Detective Jordine." Outside, however, the three entered a waiting limousine with U.S. license plates, and before Sonja knew what happened, Phil reached into his pocket, bent down behind the large vehicle, and placed something under it's back. He had done it so quickly and inconspicuously, that nobody but Sonja had noticed.

Sonja called out: “What did you do? Call the police, quickly, before they’re gone. I wrote their license number down, by the way!”

“Good! But let’s forget about the police for the moment,” Phil said, trying to simmer her down. “They’re going across the border and we want to know where? It might give us an opportunity to catch them all. I placed a beeper under their car and have in mind to follow them. We don’t want to arouse their suspicion. Besides, it’s too dangerous. I’ll keep in contact.” He gave her a quick kiss and was gone like the wind, leaving his head-shaking mate behind. For a moment she was confused, but then hurried toward their parked car.

On his own, Phil thought, ‘I used to know a supervisor here at the airport. Let me see, what was his name? Oh yes, Gerry … Gerry … ah, now I remember, Gerry Riders.’ He quickly leafed through a telephone book. After he had found the man’s number, he dialed his home and a woman answered, “Gerry is at work,” she replied, after Phil had requested to talk to him.

“I’m Detective Wilbock; Gerry was once a big help to me, and now I could use his help again. Would you be so kind and give me his number at work, please?”

“Are you the police?” she asked.

“No, I’m a private investigator,” Phil felt her reluctance to give her husband’s telephone number, so he continued, pleading with her, “Please, madam, it might be a case of life and death.”

“If you put it that way, okay then,” and she gave the detective the desired phone number, which he dialed straightaway.

“Hi, Gerry,” Phil called out with relief, “remember me? I’m the private investigator you once did a big favor for.”

“Ah, yes, Phil…”

“Philip Wilbock,” was the helping answer. “I sure could use your help this time. I just observed a kidnapping here at the airport and I need a helicopter fast. Could you get me one? I pay well.”

The supervisor answered, “Helicopter? No. But I’ve

got my own little biplane here in the hangar. Because of heavy air-traffic, though, I always need special permission to fly it. Well … I could sneak it out, I guess … but if they catch me and I lose my job."

"How about five hundred dollars?" Phil asked.

"How about a thousand?" he countered. "I take an awful chance, you know."

"Okay, okay, I'll pay. Where do we meet?"

"Where are you now?"

"Behind the big glass upstairs of the departure and arrival."

"Do you see the large hangar to your right at the end of the blacktop? I'll be in there," was the reply.

"Gee, that's more than a mile from here."

"Go below to the baggage loading of the planes and ask for Mac Sullivan; if he's free he'll drive you; we're good friends. I know all the doors are locked, but you'll find a way, Mister private eye …" He hung up, laughing.

Phil found a way all right, getting to the work crews below and thought, 'If somebody wants to plant a bomb, he wouldn't have much trouble to enter this area.'

The very first man he asked, happed to be Mac Sullivan; and he invited him into his truck without much fuss. In a few minutes they arrived at the hangar, where the driver pointed to an office, saying, "That's where you'll find Gerry." And off he drove again.

"So far so good," Phil said to himself. "Let's see how fast he can get us into the air."

"We have to keep low and hop over the fields at first," Gerry greeted him; "hopefully, you can stand this kind of turbulent flying."

"Don't worry about me," the detective told him, "I've done a few stunts with some crazy pilots."

The large hangar doors were facing away from the control tower and in that direction they made their fast takeoff, skimming low over some farmhouses. "Get me to the highway across the border, where I'll find a car with this beep detector," Phil produced a small radio-like gadget out of his pocket. "The car down there has a kidnapped girl with three men inside, to be precise, and she is drugged."

Phil was surprised when the high-pitched beep came in almost immediately, after he had turned on the receiver, indicating that the car they were following must be almost below their flight path. And soon he had found the black limousine in the southern traffic lane. “You can go higher now, I have the kidnapper’s car in my vision,” he advised the pilot.

But Phil was even more surprised when he discovered his wife with their car only fifty yards behind the limousine, while he was looking through the pilot’s binoculars. He pulled the phone out of his pocket, dialed Sonja’s number, and pretty near shouted: “What are you doing so close to the kidnappers, Sonja? You want to get yourself killed?” Then he realized how ridiculous the assumption was. They didn’t even know her. “Well, they might suspect you follow them…”

His mate interrupted him calmly, “Phil, calm down, I’m not following anybody. I don’t even know where their car is. Where are you now?”

“I’m right above you, darling,” came the relieved answer. “You see that biplane to your left, about a thousand feet up? That’s us. Stay further back, please. We don’t want any complications,” she heard his worried voice. “I’ll do the trailing from up here. Hopefully, we’re not running out of gas, before they arrive at their destination. See you, my precious assistant.”

Looking with a grin sidewards, Gerry said, “Big love, hey?”

“You better believe it,” came the sure answer.

The large limousine was easy to follow, as it turned right into a little town, where it turned left onto an overpass road across the highway.

The pilot said, “Hopefully, your kidnappers are getting to their goal soon; the sun is getting down, and I have to be able to make it back before dark; you realize that, of course.”

Phil nodded, then suddenly called out, “Oh, oh, they’re turning again, right to that large country house, see it? We’re in luck, it’s their destination. Now they park the car and turn the lights off. Fly around, please, I’ve got to get back to my wife.”

A couple of minutes later, he had Sonja on the phone again and said with joy in his voice, "We have them, darling, and know now where their house is. Stop the car there on the wide shoulder. You think you can back up slowly, to that turnoff you just passed? No, forget it. I see another turnoff to the right, about half a mile beyond the overpass. There you'll find a large and empty farmer's field. Wait there, until I call you again.

However, a highway patrol officer had watched Sonja, putting on the brakes and almost stopping, but then driving on again; so he stopped her and she thought, 'Oh, oh, what did I do now? I've got to get to that farmer's field, or Phil will wonder where I am.'

But the older and experienced policeman was very friendly and inquired, "Can I be of any help, madam? You seem to be at a loss what to do. If I can assist in some way?"

Suddenly Sonja's intuition was turned on and told her to fill the policeman in on what she and her husband, a private detective from Vancouver, were doing.

"That's a very serious matter," the policeman commented, "you're not going after them yourself?"

"No, no," she replied at once; "I honestly don't know what my husband intends to do. I'm supposed to meet him in a farmer's field at the next turnoff, but how I don't know, because he's still flying in that plane."

The highway patrol officer seemed to have an idea, and he said, "You wait there at the farmer's field, and I'll come back to you, madam. Don't do anything rash, please." Making a U-turn, he drove off.

Meanwhile, Phil was saying to Gerry, his pilot, "Mind going down on that large field and letting me off?"

He burst out: "You must be kidding! I can't..."

Phil interrupted him and said calmly, "For a thousand dollars out of my pocket, you can do it, period."

"Boy ... if something goes wrong," Gerry stuttered, "who's going to pay for the wreckage?"

Phil laughed, then said with the same calmness, "That field is as smooth as your airport; there hasn't been any rain in weeks, and the ground is solid."

"Looking at you, I see your mind is made up." Gerry

Riders gave in. "Okay, we'll look first – only a look."

"You act as if we're expecting gunfire," Phil said, laughing with a funny twist. "And what about the kidnap victim, a girl of about twenty?"

Instead of an answer and more rhetoric, the pilot swooped down for a landing, probably thinking it would be the easiest way out.

The detective pointed to a car driving into view and said, "See that approaching car there? It's my wife," his voice expressed some joy. "Try to get as close as possible to her, please."

Phil had hardly left the plane, and the anxious pilot took off again, as if some wild animal was after him.

Surprised, Sonja greeted her mate with the words, "Boy, what's with him? Was something wrong?"

"Well…" he waved his arms in the air with raised shoulders, "he was afraid to go down on this field, and we argued…" But he didn't care to elaborate.

"At least we're together again," Sonja said, while giving her husband a hug; then she moved over to let him behind the wheel. "By the way, I was stopped by the nice highway patrol officer, who thought I was in trouble and needed help. Very observant, he had seen me putting on the brakes and stopping for a moment. So, I told him what we were doing; the whole story. He was very understanding and said at the end of our conversation to wait right here. I haven't got a clue what his intentions might be, Phil."

Then the detective briefed his assistant on what he had seen from the air. "Now we know where they live. Hopefully, they don't kill the girl before we get to them."

"We, Phil?" Sonja called out with a questioning face. "You don't expect us to knock on their door…"

"Of course not," he interrupted her. "Let me do some thinking."

It had become nearly dark, when a row of headlights approached them. They were the highway patrolman, followed by three police cruisers. They all got out of their cars and encircled Phil and Sonja, who leaned against their vehicle.

After they had introduced each other, the head of the local country police, a young lieutenant, began with the words, "As we hear from our highway patrol friend, you, Mr. and Mrs. Wilbock, have been trailing these Middle Eastern folks to their house, because of their kidnapping activity, and with a kidnapped girl in their possession right now. We always wondered what they were doing up the hill in the big house, and the many strangers they receive. With the trouble you already have gone through, we have no reason not to believe you. But … there always seems to be a but!"

The officer had stopped his dialogue for a moment, and Phil couldn't help thinking, 'I have the feeling the young and inexperienced lieutenant is wiggling himself out of a job, which he thinks is not quite within the written law. Oh, I know this kind of person. They do everything by the book.'

When he heard the lieutenant again, his words were not too much of a surprise to the detective. He said, "Without real evidence, without a warrant, our hands are bound, I'm sorry to say."

Phil looked to the old highway patrolman first, then from one policeman to the other, but in the darkness could not detect their individual facial expressions. Somehow, he felt sorry for them all. Then he heard himself ask, "Did you ever hear about the Nuremberg Trials?"

One of them said, "I heard about them, but I'm not sure what it was about."

Very calmly, Phil began: "You see, gentlemen, after the Second World War in Germany, the allies – Russia, England, France and America – put the German leaders on trial in Nuremberg. Those commanders of Hitler were claiming, of course, that they had their orders and went strictly by the books, and nobody could blame them for the killings and murders. But the high international court, particularly the judges from the west, told them that there was a much higher court, away from what is taught in the physical environment, and they should've listened to it, together with their own conscience, and not to the Führer and some military books. You see this trial did not only give a message to the German leaders in the courtroom, but to all soldiers and people with authority who claim they are going by the rules or a book. The latter are very essential in our society, of course, because of the violence and lawlessness, but there are times when we have to take stock and listen to our intuition, which is soul, a superior court, if I may call it that. You understand, gentlemen?"

"I think I have an idea what you mean, sir," the lieutenant said, wishing he could get out of this situation, "but this is not the Nuremberg Trials..."

"Wait a minute," the highway patrolman snapped, "I'm not in your jurisdiction, and I'm with the detective; I think we all should go to that place. As far as I'm concerned, the evidence is there."

"You're the highway patrol..." the lieutenant began, but he was voiced out quickly by almost all the other policemen, and one of them called out, "This is our opportunity, let's go after them." Another one said, "For some time already they're a pain in our necks."

A sergeant stepped forward and asked the others, "Who's coming? I'm going. You can stay here, lieutenant, and watch the stars."

Suddenly there was action and all the policemen piled into their cruisers. That seemed to be too much for the young lieutenant, and he entered one of the cars, too.

Behind the wheel of their car and grinning toward Sonja, Phil said, "They're sent from heaven; have you any doubts about that?"

A policeman approached the Wilbocks again, and he suggested, "This time stay in the back, please, and leave the rest to us uniformed authorities." With a grin he added, "If it should come to a shootout, we have the right artillery."

Only the first car had the headlights on, when driving toward the house, where a woman answered the door. The rest became history in three minutes flat – the time the police occupied the whole building and property. Not a single shot was fired, as the surprise had worked perfectly. However, the young girl in question already had been strangled to death, upsetting Sonja and particularly Phil terribly.

Fifteen or so minutes later, when the couple walked

through the house and garden, entering a large shed in the back of the property, they discovered a long oven. Opening the iron door and poking with a rod into the ashes, Phil called out with disdain: "Here they burned the bodies. Look Sonja, remains of bones." Tears began to run down his face. "We could've prevented the girl's death. I won't forget this so easily."

Sonja put her arms around him, and so they stayed and swayed, until the noise from the house brought them back to the present.

Having found his old composure, Phil told the lieutenant, "You'll never guess what we found in the backyard shed? A long oven, suitable for burning human bodies. You'll see ... the evidence is still in the ashes. It makes me shudder."

Indeed, they had uncovered the headquarters of a kidnapping ring, and, indeed, they had burned the dead to get rid of any evidence. But their fanaticism, born of religious belief, had made them careless. Eventually a dozen more people were arrested, after the FBI had taken over the case.

The next morning, on their way back to Canada, Phil said to Sonja, "You do the driving; I've got to do some grappling with my inner self. What did we do wrong? Did we do everything right? What lessons are to be learned? Nothing is ever accidental. With you at my side now, our involvement in this kind of a crime has doubled, and so has the responsibility."

After crossing back into Canada, he surmised, speaking out loud, "Hopefully, the young lieutenant and the others got the right meaning out of my Nuremberg Trial lecture. Perhaps I should've kept my mouth shut. However, looking through a different pair of glasses, there was much validity in what I told them, and perhaps it turned them around to take action. Young people are reluctant to learn from the mistakes of the old, from our deeds and lessons. They'd rather do it all over again, often worse."

"Hey, Mister Detective," Sonja spoke up, "I'm still beside you, willing to learn, and I'm one of the young. I'm one of those who admires the old with what they think and do <u>and</u> did."

Smiling deeply with gratitude and love for her, he said, "Of course, darling. It's the young woman's death … we could've … been God? Maybe my choice was right and many innocent lives are saved." A moment later he followed it with the words, "I'm consoled by the fact that her soul lives on, getting ready for the next experience in a brand new life, perhaps not as quick ending as this one, perhaps even more violent. The law of cause and effect is calling the shots and soul will choose its next body accordingly."

Chapter 12
What The Intellect Can't Tell

Coming home from her shopping trip and putting down the bags in the kitchen, Phil could see that his mate was full of important news. She had to walk back and forth several times through the door – opening into the back of the inside garage – to empty the car. After they had been married, Phil first tried to assist her in this undertaking, but she flatly refused it by saying, "No, my husband, from now on this will be my job; that's how I see myself as a wife."

Before she began with the unpacking, however, and placing the different items into the kitchen cupboards, she joined him on the sofa in the living room. "You'll never guess who all I met at the mall."

With his usual smile, he gave her a kiss as an answer and said, "Tell me; I hardly can wait."

"First, I met Welda Eisen, and while we had a coffee and a chat, Wanda Whetherby and some of the policemen's wives joined us. A few minutes later, four more of them came and we had to move three tables together. They had a lot to discuss and it was very serious talk.

"There's over thirty women now and all want to pitch in to help the lost children and everything related to it, including the parents, of course," she continued. "They call themselves now 'The Lost and Found Children's

Mission'. During the discussion, Welda said suddenly, 'I want to join you too. I'm still healthy, have a telephone, and my doggy might do a job with me on the leash.' Well, my dear husband, I joined too." She looked at him, but only saw a grin coming her way.

A moment later she went on, "Right now our group is very concerned about the kidnapping of little kids, most of them still in the diaper stage, believe it or not. Five of them are missing at this time, as if an epidemic or something. Could it be, somebody is selling them for big money? Besides the police, the RCMP (Royal Canadian Mounted Police) has taken up the case. It's that serious."

"How come we didn't hear or read about this," he called out. "Are they trying to keep it from the public; for the time being?"

"No, Phil, no," was her immediate reply, "it only happened in the last twenty-four hours. Anyway, the women asked me to ask you, whether we want to get in on this one? One of the newcomers mentioned that it had to be without pay, so I gave her a piece of my mind, talking like that. Then you should've heard Welda; she got real angry and said, 'You don't know our Phil…' But Wanda, self-controlled as ever, never losing any temper, calmed her down again. Naturally, I offered myself to tell you of the latest in this respect and that we would do our best."

"Well, my dearest wife and assistant," he replied very seriously, "that has to be you, for the time being, because I accepted a wife and husband case an hour ago. As you know, it's our policy to do 'first come, first get', unless a real emergency should arise. And with all the police and the RCMP even showing that much interest in the case, those kidnappings are in good hands."

"I promised Welda to get her doggy at once and I also promised some of the older members to take our van, in where at least eight of us can ride, and then go snooping around, if necessary with Tom's assistance."

"Good work Sonja," he praised, then squeezed her arm. "But do remember – and you're long enough with me to know – don't let your emotions get the better of you. Use your intellect together with the voice from within – your intuition, soul."

"They'll miss you, Phil, expecting us two in the van. You mean a lot to them."

"I'll say this with deep respect, perhaps it's better that way; it'll calm some of them down. In any case, it simply can't be helped." He finished their conversation.

* * *

Walking up to a large house in one of the wealthier Vancouver districts, Phil was greeted by a butler at the door. "Follow me, please, Mrs. Hortonsen is expecting you." And he led him into a parlor, exquisitely furnished and decorated. The pictures on the walls looked like true art. 'That's what one does, when having too much money. I rather like it, though,' he thought.

An unexpected young woman entered in a rather simple dress, as if in opposition to her surrounding. Her striking blonde hair seemed to suit the rest of her slender build and make-up. She greeted the detective with a hand held out. "Although still blessed with his acquired wealth – he made a fortune during the depression – I don't go much for my grandfather's…" and she waved an arm around herself.

As if not in any rush, she continued, "I'm the only child, and inherited all this luxury, but also inherited the simplicity of my mother. Both of my parents were killed in an airplane accident six years back. Suddenly, finding myself alone, I became very lonely and depressed, unfortunately, a very common condition in today's world. As you see, I'm not hiding anything of myself, so that you might understand one of the reasons my husband left me without a trace. For him it was rather a marriage of convenience, but I looked for much more; as I still remember the wonderful and happy relationship of my grandparents, both immigrants from Finland."

She breathed deeply, then continued, "I'm willing to give him a divorce, if that's what he wants, although there never has been a divorce in our family. You see, I wanted children, but he opposed the idea adamantly. When I brought up the subject again, and then mentioned adoption, next morning he was gone without a word. This was two weeks ago and none of his friends have seen nor heard from him. I'm quite willing to come to terms, of course ... whatever he wants, even separation and divorce. Please do find him and let him know of my willingness. I don't think I frightened him into leaving because he doesn't frighten at all, and always was on top of things. Perhaps there's something else, a woman? It would not surprise me.

"For your information," she went on, "he is a member of a golf club, but I never was able to find out which one it is. He also belongs to a car racing club, where he races himself at times. All things I did not participate in, more reason for him to leave, perhaps." A moment later, she added, "And there was his very secret men's club, but I don't know a thing about it."

After Phil had left, he thought, 'By god, that woman needs help, much more than I can give. A good psychologist ... a psychiatrist ... they're probably doing more harm to her. What she needs are physical involvements, but, for different reasons than her husband has. With him it's pleasure, but with her the emotions and the heart want to get involved.'

While driving, his mind lit up suddenly and he thought, 'I should get her interested in the women's Lost and Found Children's Mission; she might do a lot of good there, healing herself at the same time.'

It took the detective only two days to find Les Hortonsen, hiding away in his men's club. Everybody was reluctant to give him information, although most of them knew where he might be. He seemed to have a lot of pull, that of a wealthy man. Finally, Phil got a tip from one of the golf course caddies, after he had bribed him with twenty dollars. Not that he simply could enter the men's club then – only true members got in – but he was able to get him on the phone. "Mr. Hortonsen, I'm not after your skin, but represent your wife as a private detective. Here is her offer: You can have a divorce. If you don't want to see her again, you can have that, too. Sooner or later, something has to give, and I'm the guy who will assist her in this endeavor."

It worked! "Okay, okay. I don't mind seeing her and she can have the divorce. But, I have one stipulation. I want you to be present, then I don't have to listen anymore to her baby talk. How about tomorrow morning at ten at her house. By the way, she can have that, too, with all the junk, and it's the last I'm going to see of that."

"Agreed. Do I meet you at the house door?"

"Agreed, Mister private eye," And he hung up.

"I found your husband, Mrs. Hortonsen, and he wants to see you," Phil told his client on the phone.

"Tell me all about it," she said, then invited him to the house.

Sitting outside in the warm sun this time, Phil began, "You asked for my honest appraisal, and I shall tell you what I thought of your husband, although we only had a short phone conversation. I think he was relieved that nothing was asked of him, only a divorce. I had the impression that he was tired of you and I doubt another woman was the reason. I had to promise him to be present tomorrow morning, when you'll meet him here. He's not afraid of you, but does not want anymore wooing you might have up your sleeve, if I may call it that. There you have it, madam. With that I went beyond my private detective's itinerary, you must understand. My intuition was the agent rather, by telling you this."

"I appreciate that very much," she said as she looked at him with a straight face. "By choosing you, Mr. Wilbock, I also listened to my intuition, going through the many listed agents in the phone book. I wonder whether we can be on a less formal relationship. My name is Mina, and may I call you Philip?"

"I have no objections … please do," he replied with a grin. "Not many of the people I know, friends and some clients, address me with Mister so-and-so. I'm too close to my fellow man. Now then, to the meeting tomorrow with your husband; you simply state your position, as you told me already, with no hidden demands."

"Of course not, Philip, I'm a woman with integrity. I'm not kidding myself; we two are simply too different, and I will have to … but that's my own private business." She seemed afraid to tell more of herself.

The meeting of the couple the next day didn't bring anything unexpected and was over in a few minutes, both sides agreeing to a quick divorce. After Les Hortonsen had left the house, Phil thought, 'They could've done that on their own without my help. However, I'm sure that my good old friend spirit, must've had something else in mind, by linking me up with this case.'

Back in the parlor, a bit later, and tea and coffee being brought in by a servant, Phil came back to the subject, he had had in his thought on the previous day. "I wonder Mina, whether you would be interested in joining a women's organization which tries to locate lost and kidnapped children. Only last year several policemen's wives have taken it upon themselves to be of help in this direction, after I had the good fortune to locate a kidnapped girl way down south in the States."

And so Philip gave her a good inside idea of what this was all about, knowing very well that things of the heart and of love might do wonders for his client. In fact, it became so successful eventually, that it made a new person out of Mina Hortonsen.

The detective also now was able to put all his mind, heart and emotions into the kidnapped babies problem, without rest.

* * *

"Something is definitely abnormal with this kidnapping case," Phil heard from his police friend, Sergeant Whetherby. "As you know, we have our own little snoopy dog now and he is as good as Mrs. Eisen's Tom, but the short trails he's following don't go anywhere. We're still checking all roads leaving town and the airport, but nothing, Phil. I tell you, the whole Vancouver police, including the RCMP, is puzzled by this kidnap business. We're not sure whether it's a ring or just very smart individuals, but we haven't got a single lead, period. The women, with their Lost and Found Children's Mission are wonderful, but their emotions are flying a bit too high, something I never could tell my Wanda, of course. Maybe you can simmer them down some, they're waiting for you to give a helping hand."

"Yes, Will, I heard some of it from my wife," the detective replied, "but I'm not a psychologist, certainly not when it comes to dozens of women. However, how can we blame them with their visibility, wanting to give radio and TV interviews, writing articles in the papers, and so forth, all of which actually might assist me, Will, because I'll take the other avenues and openings with my doggy – that is, Mrs. Eisen's Tom."

"I know that your mind works different from mine; in fact, different from all the police," the sarge allowed, then laughed. "Hey, Phil, keep me informed, will you?" And he hung up.

"I think I'll do this all by myself and let Sonja do her bit with the other girls and women," Phil said to himself. Then he thought, 'Somebody is snapping up little babies, and the way it was done, there are most likely several participants. First of all, I've got to get Tom away from the ladies, and I'm not waiting until tonight when Sonja brings him home. I'd better go to the house where their headquarters is established and have a little talk with them, along diplomatic lines, that is. I don't know why I think in those terms, as they're doing darned good work. Well, it's my innards telling me to do this on my own.'

Indeed, the Lost and Found ladies greeted him with a big 'halloo', as if he had a magic wand available and that from now on everything would be all right. 'How did I get myself into this?' he asked himself quietly. 'Perhaps I should deploy them in one direction, while Tom and I go in another.'

So, while looking at the large city map, Philip said out loud, "I presume you've been at all the warehouses, where they do the container loading, to be trucked off?" Their answer was positive.

"Well, ladies, do them again, by asking more intense questions," was his advice. "That way, the rats in the very deep holes might get the jitters and Tom and I can snoop them out. This is the best way to work, when one appears stuck. You're on the surface, and Tom and I go underground, so to speak. Don't be too irritating, though, or it might backfire."

Phil also went to one of the parents whose baby had been kidnapped, and asked for some clothing to take with him, for Tom to renew the scent all the time and remember it better. Then, tirelessly, he went to the airport and all the warehouses again, often driven on by his intuition.

Many times he carried his doggy friend, to let him have a rest and fed him little snacks of his favorite food.

At one time the detective was resting in the grass of a park, with the dog beside him for a snooze, while he contemplated. Then the cold of the darkness got them to their feet again.

Early the next morning, having given Sonja a quiet and quick kiss, the two were gone again. "I've got to do this on my own, darling," he had given an explanation to his wife the previous night. "I'll give you and the ladies a ring if I find something."

This time he drove to all the ferry terminals, which took almost half a day, but nothing.

The very last whiff Tom had gotten was at one of the container loading warehouses, so he drove there again. By now the supervisor had become very irritated, but Phil only glared at him and said, "What would you do if your baby had been kidnapped? You'd try again and again."

Then he drove to all the boat landing areas, where he met a well-remembered acquaintance, Lieutenant Henry Little George, again. "Boy, I wish I could be of help; that huge drug haul is still in my memory. Now they kidnap babies, all for a greedy return. I tell you, I sure have my eyes open here and next month we'll have our own little dog."

"Tell me, Henry, how does this whole business of loading, and the process before that, come about? Let's say I want to ship a large volume of cloth to the far east. What do I do first?" Phil asked.

"Well, as a private person, you rent or lease a container. A trucking outfit brings it to a warehouse, where it will be loaded. Some warehouses have their own containers. Then the same, or another trucking firm, brings the container here. It's that simple."

Then he amended what he was saying, "Or they truck it along the highways, wherever one wants the stuff to go."

Suddenly, Phil had an idea and he left the harbor policeman with a "Thanks a lot, see you."

While driving, he thought, 'The trucking outfits!

Perhaps I should concentrate on them.' He came upon several truck drivers, who were having their lunch outside in the sun, so he introduced himself: "I'm a private detective, investigating the baby kidnappings. It might appear strange that I come to you, knowing very well you've got nothing to do with it, but I take any lead I can get. You're driving the containers, either along the highways to their destination, or to one of the boats, anchored inside the harbor, aren't you?"

"No, our outfit has nothing to do with the waterfront; them boats are loaded by a different company," one of them answered.

Then a lady driver spoke up: "We're clean, Mister detective," and then more subdued, "that's more than we hear from other truckers."

Then a third driver had a word: "There's a lot of money to be had, and money always speaks more than it should." With a serious face he then busied himself eating the rest of his sandwich. Then he said once more, "Some go to the boats and <u>not</u> to the highways, as they should. It happens because a lot of value is at stake."

Phil said, "If I want to rent a container, it's brought to one of the warehouses where it's loaded, then you–"

One of the drivers interrupted him, "Often a container is loaded already before it comes to the warehouse. They're just having it in, pretending they're loading, and then haul it out. Most of those go to the boats and it happens often enough. And them supervisors are in on it, too. Money speaks."

"Mmm, perhaps we've got something here," Phil mumbled to himself, as he drove back once more to the container warehouse, where the dog had had his last whiff of one of the babies. But instead of going inside through the big doors, he wandered around, talking to some outside workers, particularly an elderly clean-up man, leaning on his broom, who had a lot to tell. "During all my years here, I've seen things you wouldn't believe, sir," he said. However, he also said he valued his health, and his lips were sealed, even to the police.

Walking on, Philip had to laugh to himself. 'The fellow probably thought I was an old soul, taking my dog for a stroll.' Then he came upon a couple of truck drivers, leaning against their vehicle, talking and waiting to be called into the warehouse. "I guess you guys see a lot of this country and the United States behind the wheel of your truck. Sometimes I wish I was young again, driving all over and making good money."

"Ha, ha, that you should say that," one of them replied, "just the other day I was saying something similar, but about good money, it's a juggle today. Some make it really big, and they hardly leave town, ha ha. We're not in that bracket, though."

"I guess you mean drugs?" Phil asked very naïvely.

"Not likely," one of them laughed. "Drugs are <u>not</u> shipped out of this city. It could be live material."

"You mean animals?" Phil asked with a face of surprise. "We don't have animals to sell to other countries."

They both laughed, then one of them said, "How about human animals, Mister?"

At that moment they had a radio call, and they drove off a few minutes later.

Sitting in his car again, the detective said to his doggy, "Now we know where the babies went, Tom, and we'd better hurry it up, or they'll be gone for good."

Ignoring the harbor police and the RCMP, who were in charge of observing and checking all the container loading, he went straight to the harbor master's office to find out when a single container had been loaded the day the babies had disappeared or a day later. Yes, there it had been recorded that a small freighter was loaded with only six containers, one of them heaved aboard shortly before departure.

That was it! The detective was quite sure; his intuition felt almost jubilant. But how was he to convince the police? 'Do I tell them about a dream I had?' he asked himself. 'Do I tell them about my intuition? Or some psychic ability I have? No, they never would go for that.'

Then good Tom suddenly came to his mind! Of course, he would use his doggy friend as a front, so to speak, because dogs' noses had a lot of pull in today's police work, to catch a criminal and bring a conviction.

Since the RCMP was very much engaged in this kidnap case, Philip went with Tom to their headquarters near the dock. There he was, trying to tell of his suspicion to the officer in charge, and finally said, "That small boat with the six containers aboard has the little children in one of them, I'm almost sure of it, because my dog here, equipped with one of the finest noses, has followed the trail. You can still stop that freighter, before it leaves our waters completely and is out of sight. It's our last chance, inspector."

"I don't know," he replied with disbelief. "We can't board a foreign boat that far out because of your dog's fine nose; it's simply against all rules."

'Here we go again,' Phil thought; 'he never heard of the Nuremberg Trials, and if he did, he's forgotten them.' Out loud he then suggested, "Why don't you phone Lieutenant Little George of the Waterfront Police. Because of my dog here, they had the biggest drug haul in police history."

"You mean to tell me it was <u>that</u> dog?" the inspector asked, suddenly becoming alive.

First Philip wanted to say, 'Maybe my English is not very good,' but then stopped himself. Trying to check his disgust, he finally said, "If we don't act soon, sir, they'll get away with five kidnapped babies."

Looking at the elderly detective, the inspector realized that he might've stirred an anger band in the man, who probably had much more police work and experience to show for than he ever would have. He grabbed the telephone and commanded out loud, "Get me the Coast Guard at once!" Then he gave his orders.

"I would like to be at the scene with my dog, unless you intend to open all the containers, or even search the whole boat," Phil said, very matter-of-factly, as if they couldn't do without him and Tom.

In less than half an hour they were both picked up by a large helicopter and flown out to sea. The pilot had no trouble finding the boat in question and called down through a loudspeaker – because they did not answer the radio call – that this was the Canadian police, and they had better stop at once, or else. With a grin Phil thought, 'Whatever that implies. Hopefully they'll stop and wait for our Coast Guard boat, which might take several hours.

Fortunately, though, there was a Coast Guard supply ship on its return journey from one of the weather stations at sea, and it already was visible over the horizon. In a considerably short time, Phil and Tom, together with three Mounties, were boarding the freighter.

Walking slowly from container to container, Tom's nose went to work, until he suddenly began to bark with joy; he had found his 'quarry', the little children. Opening the large door, left them all in awe. The inside looked like a house trailer, equipped with furniture and beds. And there were the five missing babies, happily playing, with two young girls looking after their welfare.

The policemen, after mounting the bridge, ordered the captain to return to Vancouver immediately, and none of his fast talk could prevent it.

With the detective and his dog aboard, the large helicopter lifted off the Coast Guard boat's deck. Patting his friend, Phil thought rather happily, 'Now I've seen everything. What will they come up with next, to line their pockets with paper gold.' Then he bent down to Tom and whispered, "We did it again. I'll be damned if we weren't guided by Spirit in this endeavor. Hopefully, we two have a few more years together."

* * *

The word of the kidnapped babies' recovery had reached shore before the helicopter sat down. Suddenly, Phil and his doggy friend found themselves surrounded by the news media, upon stepping onto solid ground again. At least a dozen reporters began to ask questions all at once. 'How will we ever get to our car?' Phil wondered, making good use of his elbow, as he tried to get through the crowd, with Tom on his arm. He shouted: "Ask the Mounties and the Coast Guard; they mounted the ship. We just happened to be with them." He was in no mood to give answers to the nosy press.

Then he saw Sonja with two ladies waving, motioning him to their nearby car. Relieved, he thought, 'Might as well ... I'll pick mine up tomorrow.' Carrying Tom, he rushed through the held-open car door, sinking back into the soft seat beside his wife. Their lips met for a moment, breathing deeply. Suddenly he felt very, very tired; the last few days of intensive detective work bore their toll on the old body. All he had in mind now was sleep, sleep, sleep, with no emotions nor thoughts stirring, but a sweet dream world would do nicely.

No words were exchange on their drive home, but upon leaving the car, he said to the ladies, "You're the greatest, and I love you. Please forgive me, but I have to rest first. In the morning I'll be okay again and we'll speak then." While Sonja opened the garage door, he turned once more to wave back.

Inside the kitchen, he simply said, "Just get me to bed, darling. No food even, please."

* * *

There was simply no way around it, Phil had to face the press or make a fool of himself; people might even think that there was something wrong with him. So he decided to have an interview on TV. He had seen this particular reporter on the air and actually liked him because his questions were always fair and well-planned beforehand.

"I don't want them in our house," he had voiced to Sonja, "so let's do it at the TV studio." This also would keep most other reporters at bay. With his doggy friend present – really the main reason for the detective's success – it worked out splendidly, although Phil found himself almost cornered twice when he had to answer what he exactly meant by intuition, inner voice and hunch. Showing his old, softening grin, he replied, "Well, if I could tell you exactly what they are and how they come about, I probably would be God. However, God I'm not; but soul and the Holy Spirit are my agents and guides. Although I'm not a church man, I believe in their authenticity and existence, and they'll help us, if we're willing to listen."

Leaving the TV studio through a back door, because of several reporters waiting outside, they drove directly to the Lost and Found Children's Mission's house, which had served as their headquarters during the time of the baby search. There, Phil and Tom were greeted with a big 'halloo', everybody wanting to squeeze and pat them, and give their thanks. After all, the detective had started them off, and they regarded him as their honorary chairman.

They had prepared an elaborate smorgasbord and, with the sunny weather outside, it was extended into the garden. This was almost like Phil's yearly garden party; in fact, many of the women knew that event only too well. If it wasn't for a few husbands present, Philip would be the only man.

To his pleasant surprise, the detective also discovered his client from a few days back, Mina Hortonsen. When she was able to get him aside for a private conversation, she commented with a thin smile, "I've begun to understand now what you and your friends stand for."

"Namely...?" Phil tried to coax her.

She seemed too embarrassed to answer him, so he said, as if it was the most assured thing in this world, "It is love, Mina! We don't mind speaking about it openly and we mean it."

Her eyes began to water and, swallowing with hesitation, she replied, "I missed out on that most of my life." Then she said, "We all watched your interview on television. I wouldn't mind asking a few more questions of what your wife also mentioned yesterday to me."

"Why don't you come for a visit tomorrow to our place," he suggested, "perhaps for lunch. I'll confer with my wife first."

"Hey, Phil," his police friend's wife, Wanda, called out with her strong voice; "we've got one of the mothers of the 'you know who' on the phone, and she would like a few words with you."

"Oh, I never was good at that," he tried to stall.

"Is it okay if we put the call on the speaker, Phil?" Wanda asked. "We're all in on this."

"Well..." he gave his permission with a motion of his hand.

"It's Mrs. Waterfield," Wanda whispered to him.

"Hi, Mrs. Waterfield," he said with difficulty, "I sure am glad you've got your little boy back."

"Now I'm crying and don't know what to say," was the

reply, "except that we love you very much and thank you with all our hearts. You gave our precious little bundle of life back to us. I simply have to tell you of our boundless gratitude." And she hung up.

Not many of the listeners were able to subdue their stirred emotions and control the flow of tears, while Phil was wiping his eyes with a hanky. After he had sat down, he finally said into the quietness, "My treasure of words is too limited ... what can I say? I just did my job."

When Mina Hortonsen came to the Wilbocks next day for lunch and a chat, she greeted them with the words, "I find it difficult to explain, what the last few days have done to me, getting to know all those wonderful ladies. And why? Because my husband disappeared."

Laughing, Phil explained, "Nothing is ever accidental, Mina, and you yourself can learn to direct everything in your life. My wife will tell you."

"She did already, one of the reasons I'm here."

"During the few days with us, you experienced love," Phil said, as he led her into the living room; "divine love, that is." After they had seated themselves, he continued, "Recognition and initiative – often many years apart – came to you in quick succession, indeed a rarity in today's society of know all. I'm sure you'll make the most of it."

"If you only knew under what circumstances Phil and I met," Sonja said as she sat down beside the visitor. "And today, after only a few months with him, I'm a brand new person. It's not only because of our love for each other, but of what we know, experience, believe and trust in. The meaning of my life has been reversed by one hundred and eighty degrees and more. Can you believe that?"

"Hey, hey, my beloved wife," Phil said as he got up, "you're confusing our guest. Let's eat first and then delve into the unknown."

Grinning to herself, Sonja thought, 'She's confused already, if pleasantly, and my words don't add much to that.' Then her thought train went on, 'Now I'm anxious myself as to what he'll say about the unknown.'

'Delving into the unknown?' the visitor thought,

aroused by an impassioned question. ‘I wonder what Philip will come up with next?’

While walking into the large kitchen, Mina Hortonsen thought, ‘Only a week ago I was so terribly distraught, and look at me now! Undeniably a new life has come into my vision.’

E N D

This novel will be followed by
2999 Adler Street II

www.ingramcontent.com/pod-product-compliance
Ingram Content Group UK Ltd.
Pitfield, Milton Keynes, MK11 3LW, UK
UKHW041846190726
13854UKWH00002B/749